Akim and the Night Intruders

Akim and the Night Intruders

Rita F. Kurian

Akim and the Night Intruders

Cover of book and illustrator: Vandana Pavamani

Published by
Lighthouse Christian Publishing
SAN 257-4330
5531 Dufferin Drive
Savage, Minnesota, 55378
United States of America

www.lighthousechristianpublishing.com

Chapter 1
The Strange Intrusion

Night was falling on a cool October evening as fireflies flitted around through tall trees and long green grass in Dora Valley. The trees whispered in the soft breeze and shadows stretched over the rolling hills. The valley was alive with sounds of little frogs croaking near pools of water looking their night hunt of mosquitoes and insects. Crickets chirped merrily hopping in the grass. Thousands of stars lit up the sky while the night-lights in the valley flicked on all over. The field mice scuttled around looking for nighttime grain while wild brown bunnies and rabbits leaped around the forested hills of Dora Valley.

Akim was hurrying home with his torch lighting up his narrow pathway, when just then Mrs. Lama had caught sight of Akim out of her cottage window and called out to him frantically. "Akim, hurry, hurry come here!"

Akim looked towards Mrs. Lama's cottage and spotted her face peering at him anxiously from her window. He rushed towards her cottage, wondering what had happened, wondering if a snake was in her cottage. The last time he went by Mrs. Lama's cottage, she was screaming "snake, snake" and the neighborhood ran in with sticks to chase out the black grass snake that quietly slithered back to the forest.

Mrs. Lama, a huge lady, wearing a moss-green Baku, (long dress tied in the middle) her hair tied in an enormous bun with crinkly black eyes, said, "I got something for you, and Aunt Nelly and Uncle Jon." She handed Akim a hot packet. Mrs. Lama had been on a momo-making spree, (stuffed dumplings) and was anxious to send some for her good friend, Aunt Nelly. Akim took it gladly, relieved there was no snake in her house.

"Thank you ma'am" he said politely.

Mrs. Lama said, "I know you like momos too, I had promised Aunt Nelly I was going to bring them. I was planning to take a walk down and give them, and now I spotted you, so you can take them. Now just wait a moment and have a bowl of hot soup."

Akim said, "Thank you Ma'am but it is getting dark, and I have to be home or Uncle Jon and Aunt Nelly will be really worried, it is already night."
Mrs. Lama insisted, "It won't take a moment Akim. This is a wonderful evening, with the fireflies and the stars out! I feel like taking a little walk. I was just going to go down to your cottage, I am sure your walk down to your cottage will be beautiful, only I hate those black grass snakes, ugh!"

Akim nodded and said, "I like the walk down but Aunt Nelly gets very worried the minute it is dark."

Akim gulped down his soup, said thank you and hurried down the foot pathway to his farm cottage where he lived with his aunt and uncle. Akim had lost his parents to an accident when he was a baby and his aunt and uncle brought him up as their own child. He was a 12-year-old boy, had a pale face with sad, dark brown eyes and a mop of thick brown hair.

Oh no, thought Akim in dismay, "*It's getting dark and I bet Aunt Nelly will be mad at me!*

Just as Akim turned around the corner in the path, he stiffened. Ahead of him was a little bonfire cracking on dead twigs and leaves lit by Don, the school bully and his friends. Don was 17 years old, tall, thick set with spiky black hair, bull's neck, sharp black eyes, skin burned brown with all his outdoor activities and thin straight lips. His friends Soki, Jo and Nok stood looming in the shadows, menacing and jeering. Akim hurried past them hoping Don would ignore him, but Don was not the kind of boy to let a day go by without ragging any boy or girl. Don started singing aggressively and loudly, "The young fool walks by, under the night sky!" Then, Akim felt tiny stones pelting him. One of the stones pelted him very sharply and Akim saw blood coming out of his arm. Akim stopped on his tracks and said yelled bravely "Stop that!"

Don mockingly jeered, "Stop or not, then what, what can you do little boy?"
Akim did not answer and walked by, frowning, his forehead furrowed, angry at his own helplessness.

Don called out after him, "Survival of the fittest, the weak ones fall down!"
Akim called back bravely, "Sometimes the little ant bites the big elephant's ear and brings him down!" to which Don and his friends roared with laughter yelling, "You are an ant for sure, little Akim, go crawl into your anthill."

Trembling, Akim hurried down the valley the flickering lights from the cottages lighting up his pathway. He finally reached the farmhouse with relief. The thick scent of ginger flowers around the farmhouse smelt delicious, the farm cottage glowing with lights looked very warm and welcoming and as Akim swung open the gate, Aunt Nelly was already standing in the veranda looking very concerned and said, "Akim, you know I want you to come home before dark. Come on, hurry in, dinner is ready!"

Akim said meekly, "Aunt Nelly, Mrs. Lama sent us some momos, that is why I got a little late, sorry, I know you hate be coming home in the dark."

Aunt Nelly exclaimed, "Oh, okay, that happens sometimes, so you are forgiven. Now, that is very sweet of Mrs. Lama to send us momos. She had told me she would make some and bring them home, but I never expected her to send them today. Now that's great, we can have them along with dinner!"

Akim, Aunt Nelly and Uncle Jon settled down at the dining table to eat a piping hot dinner of chapatti (flat bread) vegetables, roasted chicken, lentils with the addition to Mrs. Lama's delicious momos. In fact, there was far too much to eat that night with the addition of the momos.

The farmer was a tall man with a thick mob of black hair. He looked more like a scientist than a farmer with a very high thoughtful forehead, kind wise eyes, and a very calm nature. His wife was tall and slightly plump, had lively sparkling eyes, humorous and generous. She was a kind-hearted vibrant woman involved all kinds of good work in their little valley.

After dinner, Uncle Jon, Aunt Nelly and Akim sat around a flickering fire. Aunt Nelly looked at Akim and said, "Akim, you are very quiet, is everything okay?"

Akim replied, "Yes, I'm fine Aunt Nelly" and said no more. He sat near the fire, musing about the day, frowning again, and thinking of Don thinking gloomily *would Dan and his friends keep trying to bring me down, and for how long?* Suddenly he heard Uncle Jon saying something to him and he started saying, "Oh, yes, Uncle, what was it?"

Uncle Jon smiled at Akim and said, "You are thinking of something, get it off your chest, talk about it boy, it is always better to speak about something rather than bottling it up."

Akim shook his head, trying to be brave, and not wanting to make his uncle and aunt worried and said, "I am good, Uncle, nothing is wrong, just tired, can I go to bed now?"

Uncle Jon said, "Sure, go ahead, sleep tight and hope the bugs don't bite!"

Akim laughed weakly, not really amused, and Aunt Nelly watched him carefully as he made his way out. As Akim walked out, he heard her say to Uncle Jon with deep concern in her voice, "Something is wrong with our boy, not sure what is bothering him. He bottles up everything, never tells us what he is thinking, he tries to be brave. I know he is a brave wonderful boy, who deserves much more than he gets. I wish he would get some good friends, half his troubles would be over with having friends!"

Uncle Jon said, "True, but there is a time for everything, I believe Akim is going through a season, and he will come out of it better!"

Aunt Nelly sniffed and said, "I hope you are right, I don't want anything to happen to Akim!"

Akim thought, *Aunt Nelly is right, I need good friends and I have none right now, great going for me…*

Later, Aunt Nelly made her way to Akim's room and she sat at the edge of his bed and asked him worriedly, "Akim is everything okay?"

Akim nodded "Yes, Aunt Nelly, I am fine, just a little tired, wanted to sleep early!"

Aunt Nelly said, "Well, you look a little down, come on, tell me, child, I know something is not quite right."

Akim shook his head and said, "I'm fine, Aunt Nelly."

Aunt Nelly said, "Come on Akim, don't hide anything from me, I am here to help you. I will never scold you if you tell me the truth, hiding things can only make them worse most of the time!"

Akim finally reluctantly told his aunt, "Today, some bullies had grabbed my lunch. They are bullying many younger children as well. Every day, they grab things, push us to the ground and even beat up some of the younger children. Everyone is afraid of them, as they are far stronger. Don, their leader is Mr. Loki's nephew. You know how everyone always listens to Mr. Loki, as he is so rich and powerful. Right now, as I was walking down the valley pathway, Don and his friends were pelting stones at me!"

Aunty Nelly clucked her tongue, shook her head disapprovingly, and said, "All so wrong, I am going to deal with it straight away tomorrow morning, I am very upset about the bullies and I am going to meet the school authorities tomorrow and talk to them regarding this bullying."

Akim said, "No, don't Aunt Nelly, Don is related to Mr. Loki and Mr. Loki will make more trouble for us."

Aunt Nelly snorted and said, "Let me see what Mr. Loki can do to us, Uncle Jon and I will never let anything bad happen to you or our home, believe me, I am going to deal with Don and the others, Mr. Loki will have to watch out for us, not the other way around!"

Akim said anxiously, "Aunt Nelly, you are very brave; I know you fear nothing, but please be careful. Everyone in Dora Valley knows Mr. Loki is trouble if anyone apposes him. I think the matter will settle on its own. Please leave it."

Aunt Nelly pursed her lips and said firmly, "Let us see tomorrow, now goodnight, dear Akim, and don't think about it. Let tomorrow come. Each day has its own problems so let us take it one day at a time. Akim, bullying simply is not right. Do you want to know a secret Akim, in the heart of every bully, is really a coward? To hide their fears, they attack others. As long as people are silent, the bullies think they won the battle, but they really can't win the war. If their bullying is addressed, they can change and become better children many times."

"What war, Aunty Nelly?" asked Akim, surprised.

Aunt Nelly answered slowly, "The bigger things in life. They lose out on that; they have lost the big picture."

Akim thought about that silently. He liked the idea of the bigger picture; it spoke of higher purposes and made him feel linked to something greater. He said

meekly to Aunt Nelly, "I like the idea of the bigger picture; perhaps you should report the bullying."
Aunt Nelly patted him and said, "It is wired in your brain that you have a destiny for greater things, but how, when, where was the big question. You are not an ordinary boy, my child. I am waiting to see something great come out of you! You think about things not many in your age do!"

Akim answered slowly, "I guess we all have some mission to do something great, but we have to look for it, discover it, I think many times we may miss it if we are not looking for it!"

Aunt Nelly exclaimed, "This is why I say you are a thinking child. You think so deep into everything, and this is why greatness will come to you!"

Akim felt slightly better after that conversation. Aunt Nelly said a prayer with him, tucked him in bed, and switched off the light. Akim did not fall asleep immediately. Thousands of thoughts were pounding his mind. He thought, "I will take it one step at a time, and hope things will get better by tomorrow. The sun will always come out the next day, Aunt Nelly and Uncle Jon are the greatest, I am so lucky!" Akim looked out of his window, half-asleep and suddenly jolted wide-awake for a moment. He sat up and stared out of the window puzzled, there seemed a strange light in the sky, white and glowing.

"Strange," he thought, "must be some sort of star…it looks the brightest I have ever seen." He yawned and then kept looking out sleepily into the sky and slowly his eyes closed and he fell into a deep sleep, dreaming he was flying in the sky.

He was deep in sleep until about 2:00 a.m. Suddenly, he awoke with a jolt, startled; he looked around a little scared, wondering what awoke him. He was aware of a great brightness out in the garden.

"What is it?" he whispered to himself, a little nervous, but still stoic inside, deciding he was not going to panic. He said softly to himself, "This light seems to be linked to that bright light I saw before sleeping, it is all so strange. I must see if Uncle Jon and Aunt Nelly are okay." Akim stepped out of his warm bed into the freezing room. He wrapped his warm woolen dressing gown around him because of the icy cold temperature at that hour of night. He then heard a familiar yet untimely sound, "Mow, mow, mow!"

Akim exclaimed loudly amazed, "Why, the cows in the farm are mooing, why a cow at this time!"

A few seconds later, he heard another sound, "Meow, Meow, meow." Goldie, the farm cat was very agitated cat as she ran around the farmhouse, looking very frightened and confused. She shot into the drawing room like a streak of lightning and then a ball of fury. Akim almost felt like chuckling when he saw her running around so frightened, yet at the same time was very concerned. Something was terribly wrong. Outside, in the farm, the three German Shepherds, Bruno, Brutus, and Brandy started barking furiously. The hens clucked around madly, and a few goats were bleating painfully.

Akim set out determinately to Uncle Jon and Aunt Nelly's bedroom. He had to check if they were all right. Then he heard a horrible sound. He stopped still in his tracks, suddenly chilled with fear. The sound of eerie bloodcurdling howling started.

"The wolves!" thought Akim in fear. All the people in Dora Valley dreaded the ravenous wolves that lived in the mountain forests near the valley! Some people told terrible stories about wolves around the valley, which made everyone shiver with fear. Sometimes, these wolves would come to farmlands and steal sheep, goat and hens.

Akim told himself fiercely, "I am not going to chicken out, I am going to see if Uncle and Aunt are okay, and you rotten wolves and bright lights are not going to scare me now."

He remembered his aunt telling him once whenever one is afraid; they should sing a happy song. He tried to remember a song he had learnt from Aunty Nelly and with great effort, started humming it.

"When fear knocks on my door
I will sing a happy song
Inside, I will become strong
All fears will flee far away
Faith will fill my heart
All along the way!"

As Akim continued to hum, the howling did not seem so fearsome and eerie. Akim started to feel braver and set out purposefully to Uncle Jon and Aunt Nelly's bedroom. As he stumbled across in the dark, he heard thumping sounds in the front room, and as he came close, he found it extremely dark because the thick curtains were drawn. He could barely see anything in the drawing room, and he groped around for a switch to turn on the lights.

Suddenly he realized something was walking in the dark. It was breathing rather heavily. Akim's heart pounded and he stood still again and he felt a chill going down his spine and tried to shout, "Help" but found his throat stuck and garbled.

That creature moved softy towards him and touched him. Akim let out a yell and the creature in the dark yelled out too. "Who is that?" shouted the creature.

Akim was relieved and exclaimed, "Oh Uncle, it was you, what a relief! What happened? The wolves are howling!"

Uncle Jon said, "Wondering the same thing here Akim. The animals are disturbed."

Uncle Jon drew the curtains and both Uncle Jon and Akim gasped with amazement for as they drew the curtains, they saw the countryside lit up with a cool silvery light. Akim said, "Uncle, this is really weird, shall we go out and see?" Akim felt braver now that Uncle Jon was with him.

Just then, Aunt Nelly walked into the drawing room and she gave a little scream exclaiming, "Oh great guns and robbers!" "What is happening to our Dora

Valley? Why is it so bright? Why are the animals agitated? Call the neighbors!   Call the police! Oh help!"

Aunt Nelly was usually very brave but today, she looked very fearful. She sat down suddenly in a flurry with her heart beating wildly.   After a few moments, she got up and looked out of the window. As they looked out, they were amazed to see the neighbors awake. All lights were on in Dora Valley as all the valley people peered out of their windows, shocked. Everyone was clearly afraid, wondering why the animals were disturbed and why there was this strange silver light.

Uncle Jon suddenly said, "I'm going out to see what it is!"

"NO!" screamed Aunt Nelly, "Don't do it, you don't know what it is!"

Akim remarked humorously, "Aww Aunt Nelly, this is not like you, you are usually the first one to investigate!"

Aunt Nelly gave a little weak laugh and said, "Sometimes, it's better to be safe than sorry!"

Uncle Jon replied, "Perhaps that is true, but tonight is not that night. Sometimes we have to step out and take that chance. This is our house, we have to protect it, we might get hurt, and our animals may get hurt. We can't leave it just like that. See, the neighbors too are awake, we are not entirely alone."

The farmer's wife shuddered. Then Akim asked timidly, "Can I come too Uncle?" As he expected, Aunt Nelly protested heatedly with a big resounding "NO, NO! Bad enough your uncle is going you stay here. Basically, I can see nothing out there even though it is just so bright, it is strange." She peered out of the window and Akim joined her, scanning the countryside keenly.

"Wait," gasped Akim excitedly, "I see something, I see something!"

"Great guns and robbers, what is it?" cried his Aunt.

"Near the trees in the garden, I see a figure!" As they looked, they spotted a figure standing near the trees. The figure emanated a queer silver sheen. It was tall and thin and stood still. It seemed to have two legs, two arms and a face!

"I will deal with it!" said the farmer grimly. "This can't do any harm to my livestock or us. I will not let it. This is my farm, my house, my family, it can't harm us." He picked up a fat stick he kept in the house and started to walk out with a newfound courage. There was no stopping him. Akim thought of a poem he once read:

> *When a frumpy creature*
> *Knocks on your door*
> *Drive it out with a mighty roar*
> *Don't let it trample on your floor*
> *Drive it out*
> *It will run far away*
> *It will never find itself*
> *To come by your place*
> *Any other day!*

As Uncle Jon marched bravely out of the house, several neighbors got courage and stepped out slowly, standing in their gardens.

Breathlessly, they watched the farmer walking to the creature and the creature just seemed to watch the farmer without moving.

Mr. Mundy, the principal of a school yelled out, "Careful Jon, don't venture out, you don't know what it is, it might attack you!"

Ms. Lama heard the commotion and came running down the valley to see what had happened, her eyes wide with fear as she stood near the valley folk.

Uncle Jon raised his hand and said, "I got with prayers and faith that nothing will happen to me."

Aunt Nelly shook her head and muttered, "Not wise, no, no, now this is not the wise thing to do!"

Uncle Jon walked on bravely towards the creature and as he came closer, the creature looked at the farmer very intently. The neighbors watched anxiously as if a drama was unfolding before them. Aunt Nelly covered her eyes, and started praying. Akim watched with bated breath and slowly edged closer to Uncle Jon. Aunt Nelly did not see Akim going because she had covered her eyes. Akim stood bravely behind Uncle Jon. He did not want any harm to come to Uncle Jon, and he thought bravely, I will be here to cover his back!

Uncle Jon was now directly before the creature and he said called out boldly, "Who are you and what do you want?"

The creature stepped forward. The people could clearly see its face now. It glowed incandescently with silvery light. It had a thin face with a pointed nose and a silver beard. Its eyes shone brightly, but its face surprisingly did not look menacing.

As Uncle Jon went forward, the creature stepped forward. Then to everyone's amazement, several other creatures stepped forward, all glowing with silvery light. In total, there were around seven of them! Whew! Everyone nearly whistled out aloud stunned.

All the town people gasped thinking, "What did they want! Were these aliens that finally came down on Earth?"

Mr. Loki, an enormous man with shaggy black eyebrows, hooked nose and lips always veered to a sneer, the richest man in town stood among the neighbors and he said loudly, "Star Wars, the aliens have come to capture us, hide, run for your lives!" Though Mr. Loki said that, he made no effort to run himself. However, everyone stepped back nervously. Mrs. Loki stood nervously next to Mr. Loki a thin, frail woman with rabbit teeth chattering with fear. She looked up at Mr. Loki and asked him worriedly, "Did you take your pressure tablet this morning?"

Mr. Loki answered her impatiently, "Yes, yes!" wondering what his pressure tablets had to do with the aliens. Mrs. Loki added timidly, "I don't want your pressure to shoot up seeing all these aliens." Mr. Loki grunted.

In the meantime, Aunt Nelly uncovered her eyes and was horrified to see Akim standing behind Uncle Jon. She clucked her tongue saying, "Akim did not listen, I told him not to go!" With that, she then made her way towards Uncle Jon and Akim, and held on to the wicket fence. After a moment, she took a deep breath and stepped forward boldly reminiscent of her very bold soul. "Dear Creatures," she began in a shrill quivering voice, "What, may I ask are you and where do you come from?"

Uncle Jon murmured nervously, "Nelly, step back, I am handling this!"
Then to their surprise, one of the tall silver men came forward and spoke to them in a voice that reminded everyone of silver rain. His eyes had a twinkle. On

looking at him, everyone felt he was a kind-good-natured fellow.

"Hi, my name is Starrho." he said, "We live beyond the silver stars and we are called the Star Men.

Mr. Loki stepped forward and said triumphantly, "Ha, I told you it was Star Wars; these creatures have come to invade us on earth and make us slaves!" Mr. Loki said it as if he was enjoying the idea. Aunt Nelly glared at him.

Starrho continued politely, "We have come to Earth on a mission. A strange mission it is. The Great One beyond the stars is concerned about Earth. Earth is losing something very precious, and unless someone performs this task, a great calamity will fall upon the Earth."

The town folks gasped and stared in wonder. As Starrho was speaking, Akim's heart was strangely warm. He felt something very important was about to happen and he felt like speaking with them.

Just then, Aunt Nelly interrupted a little nervously as she felt she had to do or say something to ease the confusion she was feeling. Aunt Nelly felt she had to do something reassuring at this time of strange unsettling events. Tea was a comfort drink and she seized a chance to offer everyone tea.

"Fellows, do you want some tea?" She asked. The Star Men stared at her and one of the Star Men asked, "T? What is that?"

Everyone was rather amused that Aunt Nelly had chosen that moment to ask if the visitors would like some tea and Mr. Loki snorted rudely muttering "Silly woman, just like her to ask something ridiculous at the eve of Star Wars! Mr. Loki sounded as if he liked his idea that this was an Earth invasion and felt it lent some excitement into his mundane existence. Uncle Jon raised an eyebrow and said inquiringly "Nelly, tea at a time like this?"

Mrs. Lama said hurriedly, "I think tea is a good idea, will calm us down. I will help you dear we will make the tea. Some other ladies said, "Tea is a good idea" their knees weak and trembling walked gingerly to Aunt Nelly's kitchen to make tea. Mrs. Loki coughed loudly as if she too thought it was a good idea but was too afraid of Mr. Loki to say so! The Star Men gravely shook their heads and one of them said, "Our drink and food is not of this world."

"Well, you just don't know what you are missing," retorted Aunt Nelly with a little nervous laugh, trembling a little though she did not want to show anyone she was afraid. She went busily to her kitchen while several of the women joined her ready to make tea for the waiting anxious valley folk. Akim was secretly wondering whether these strange Star Men would suddenly pounce on them and gobble them up!

Mr. Loki said softly to the others, "I think I should get out my shotgun hidden in my house."

Uncle Jon shook his head and answered, "They don't look venomous, no need to Mr. Loki."

The Star Men smiled sweetly at all of them, and Mr. Loki said softly and excitedly to those standing around him, "I see a strange nasty gleam in their eyes!"

Akim stared at them solemnly thinking, *Well, they seem to have kind eyes, I don't think they could harm us*!

The Star Men could sense the turbulence in the people and Starrho said calmly, "Now, let me introduce us all," "Meet Dendal, Zora, Billho, Grinko, Piran, and Roko. We are sorry we had to upset your night with this rude awakening. We know you Earth people are in the deepest sleep at this hour of the morning, 3 a.m., but this is the time we had to come."

Some of the other said politely said "Hi!" while a few others stared stonily at the Star Men. Then they all sat down on the green lawn while Aunt Nelly along with the other women brought tea and buttered toast, which they set on a little table in the lawn. People helped themselves to the tea and toast. Aunt Nelly brought out a huge gigantic mat on the lawn as she noticed the cold dawn dew was settling on the grass and everyone was shivering in the dampness.

They sat down gratefully on the mat, and ate toast and drank hot tea, sitting under the stars gazing in wide-eyed wonder at the Star Men sans some of the disgruntled in the valley.

Akim thought, *I always wanted a midnight feast, well here it is, kind of exciting!*
The animals had suddenly become peaceful and calm. Though they had initially been perturbed by the night invasion with strange glowing lights and the presence of a different entity, they sensed the presence of the Star Men

was not a menacing one. The wolves had stopped howling. A sudden peace descended over the valley.

As they sipped their tea, Uncle Jon asked the Star Men, "Now please tell us what has caused so much flurry and worry for Earth, what is this mysterious treasure that the Earth has lost?"

Chapter 2
The Star Men Talk

While the others sipped tea, watching the Star Men warily, Starrho, the very tall noble looking Star Man with glowing eyes and a thin face with a long sharp nose looked at them and said gravely, "As I said, something the Earth once had is now lost. The Great One beyond the stars looks down and is very sad. The Earth is getting darker and darker. The lie has become the truth, and the truth a lie. This is the worst stage Earth could get into…it is nearing its self-destruction and the people don't realize it or even want to listen."

"Who is the great one?" asked Akim, picturing a warrior Star Man sailing the skies. He glanced up in the sky expectantly and the others followed suit, staring up at the sky.

The other Star Man, Dendal, known as the wise Star Man who had a calm serene face with huge glowing eyes said, "The Great One is the One who made everything, including the stars and the universe. He watches everything and He is very concerned about the people on Earth. Unless something is recovered back to Earth, there will be mass destruction on the Earth. The dark one is rising, his hour has come, but many people on Earth are actually revolting against the Great One, scorning Him and because of this, they have rejected the only protection they could have against the one who sends destructive works. The hour has come of the greatest deception in the history of Earth!"

Akim thought to himself, *I hear what the Star Men are saying, something worse than ever is happening; and yet no one is noticing it. Each night on the television, I watch the news of terrible things happening all over Earth, people killed in unimaginable ways. I hear of wars in other lands all the time, and looting, burning, kidnapping. Yet in Dora Valley, people see it but are content with everything. Nothing really worries them because it is all so far away from them and they feel so safe!*

Dendal smiled at Akim, it seemed Dendal read his thoughts and Akim thought in wonder, *Wow, I think he just read my thoughts!*

Dendal said gently, smiling at Akim, "I don't always invade into people's thoughts, but sometimes, the Great One lets me listen to people's thoughts if I need to know something. Yes Akim, you got it...terrible things are happening all over the world!"

Akim exclaimed, "Amazing, I listen to the news every evening and it haunts me sometimes, too terrible!" The others stared blankly. They did not understand what Akim or Dendal was speaking about.

Don bristled up looking very angry and said scornfully to his friends, "How dare that worm Akim speak to the alien, Akim that small rotten useless good for nothing speaking to that alien and why is that alien giving him importance by speaking to him?"

Don's friends nodded in agreement and Akim heard that comment and turned red hot.

Mr. Loki, Don's uncle cleared his throat and said loudly, "Why is Akim speaking about the news beats me, the boy does not really understand anything. Poor miserable creature, he should be in bed now anyway. Aliens, we are safe in Dora Valley and the news is far away!"

Mrs. Singh, a schoolteacher chirped in saying, "Yes, the news is terrible with all the horror happenings, but we are safe here in Dora Valley. I am so glad we are tucked in a safe place!"

"What is lost?" asked Mr. Mundy, principal of the best school in Dora Valley called Learners and Conquerors. Mr. Mundy was a small man, energetic, powerful and eloquent.

"A great treasure is lost," repeated Dendal, the wise Star Man.

"Treasure?" echoed the valley folk.

Mrs. Lama asked in interest, "Are some bags of gold and jewels lost somewhere on Earth?"

Mr. Loki said softly to Mrs. Loki, "I need to get hold of the treasure and I am annoyed that these silly aliens mentioned about it opening. I could have gone alone and got it and now everyone will want it too!

Mrs. Loki wrung her hands nervously and looked around hoping no one had heard Mr. Loki.

Starrho said gently, "No, not earthly treasure. It is something far more precious than jewels. Jewels are temporary treasures that can get lost or stolen and is useful for a period only. That which is lost is something far greater and its loss is making the Earth darker and darker."

"Greater treasure, what can it be? Darker and darker?" queried Mr. Loki, "How is that so? The Earth seems quite bright to me, the sun is shining so bright and the moon too…the world is as bright as it could be, and anyway, no treasure is greater than jewels and gold!"

Dendal, the Star Men replied, "Dear Man, you are wrong, jewels and gold will not help you when you face the darkness and death, and this darkness I speak of is not the darkness without the sun. It is another kind. It covers the Earth like a blanket with a few bits of streaming light here and there, but darkness rages getting worse by the hour."

His words sounded strange and sinister and everyone trembled a little. Many of the valley folk thought of different things, Aunt Nelly thought of Akim's bullies and Uncle Jon suddenly thought of the evening news, and others thought of horrors and terrible nightmares.

Dendal continued, "This darkness is hatred, envy, malice, murder, violence, lies, gossip, slander, and thieving. All over the world, it is rising by the day. Many people are distressed and living in fear and people can no longer trust each other, nations and even families are falling apart!"

"We are quite happy here in Dora Valley and we all have happy families!" broke in Aunt Nelly a little indignantly, "I mean things are happening, there, but we are here, and we are quite safe and in the end, that's all that matters isn't it?"

Roko, another Star Man with a sharp pointed nose who was known as the investigator, the detective Star

Man said who usually found out secrets said, "Ah, maybe so, you are quite okay in Dora Valley, but you perhaps are not aware that in different parts of the Earth strange bad things are happening. I sometimes travel all over the Earth, and see terrible things. My dear people, now this darkness is spreading, it is advancing to Dora Valley too, there will come a time when no one is in a safe comfort zone anymore, not even you, unless you do something about it!"

Aunt Nelly listened silently and said in a low voice to Uncle Jon, "I can't imagine Dora Valley getting bad. Besides of course some annoying people and a few bullies and some other irritating folks, things were quite good in Dora Valley, everyone is happy and comfortable."

"So what will you do about it, what is your mission?" asked Uncle Jon wondering when the Star Men would get down to the point. Uncle Jon usually communicated everything he needed to in a few short sentences and he personally felt the Star Men were rotating around the topic.

Starrho replied, "The Great One looked over the Earth, and saw one who is small, but lionhearted and He said, "This Earth One will do the task, I have chosen him." So now, we need the help of the Earth one to do the task along with us. We need to take him along with us."

"What task and who are you planning to take, defiantly I hope not anyone from Dora Valley, we are simple good people and we don't want any trouble, we mind our own businesses and help our folks who need it. Please spare us from any trouble!" said Uncle Jon a little alarmed.

Starrho cleared his throat delicately and said, "The Great One sent us to get the Earth One, we need to take him with us to accomplish the task."

The valley folk looked puzzled. They wondered how they could help, and who among them could possibly help the Star Men. They were as Uncle Jon has said simply valley folks, who lived in their little town, sharing and caring. They minded their own businesses, stuck out their noses for each other in times of trouble. Overall, they were a happy simple-hearted lot. None of them seemed created for great worldly earthly heroic stunts of saving the Earth and helping The Great One, whoever He was.

Mr. Loki always felt he was destined for great things. He said conceitedly, "I think the aliens would choose me, I am the greatest and the best in Dora Valley! At the same time, Mr. Loki did not care about what was happening in the world around him. He would often say to Mrs. Loki when they listened to the evening news on the television, "These rotten people brought all that destruction on themselves; stupid, not wise, not clever, now let them suffer!" Mrs. Loki would nod and say, "Yes dear!" though secretly she felt a little sorry for the people suffering all over.

Mr. Loki cleared his throat importantly, hoping that they would say they had chosen him for the mysterious task, but the Star Men did not answer him. "Er Er, I think…." Mr. Loki said. The Star Men did not seem to hear him and he felt snubbed. He looked down mumbling some unmentionable things to himself.

"I think you got the wrong town," said Shaan, the beautiful 17-year-old in the valley. Shaan had long straight silky jet-black hair and beautiful eyes with a delicate sharp nose. Shaan, the belle of the town was to go and attend a beauty pageant held in Dora Valley and she wanted nothing to step in the way of her well-ordered plans. Most of the people in Dora Valley was certain she would win, and Shaan had no doubt about it.

Shaan continued, "We are people who enjoy our lives, are happy and do not harm anything, I think you should go to the heart of the muddle in the Earth. We definitely are not in that muddle!"

Dendal the Star Man said understandingly, "I know you do not put to put yourself in a puddle and be in that muddle, but the Great One's eye has fallen on Dora Valley. We call this great destiny, someone is chosen for a task in spite of his or herself. The only thing is, is that person willing to do it? If not, the task falls on someone else, or otherwise if no one is down it, it changes the history and destiny of the Earth in an unfavorable way. Are you willing folks in Dora Valley to step in and help?"

Shaan did not like the idea of "stepping in and helping", and she said a little haughtily tossing her head, "I think the Great One has made a mistake, check out another town!"

"The Great One never makes mistakes," said Zora, another Star Man. Zora was the most adventurous Star Man. He had traveled all over the Earth on many missions, he was not as tall as the others were, he had bright eyes, with lips that curved up with merriment and his curly hair glowed like silver fire. He looked very friendly and energetic.

Mr. Loki said a little loudly and rudely, "Everything is written in the stars, destiny is already chalked out for every human, destiny will happen, nothing can change it, so no one can do anything to change it, but I believe I am destined for great things."

"Some things will happen that are meant to happen, true," replied Dendal quietly, "However, you are earthbound, so you can't understand that destiny is not king. It has no real hope. Destiny is not the ultimate end of the road for humans. Right decisions and choices change our lives. Destiny can be very dampening if someone is destined for something sad. We can stop a bad destiny by a right choice and the Great One helps us too when we ask Him!"

The townsfolk kept silent because they were in great awe of these shining Star Men who even spoke to them of such high bizarre things.

Mr. Loki gave an impolite snort and said, "Bah!" That night, Mr. Loki felt ignored by the others. He wanted them all to disagree with the Star Men and send them on their way and was very uncomfortable with their presence. He looked at the others and said, "These aliens are talking rubbish, I just hope they are not trying to invade the Earth and take us as their slaves."

The Star Men did not contradict Mr. Loki and kept looking at the others. No one seemed to notice Mr. Loki or answer him, infuriating him further.

Starrho continued grandly as if Mr. Loki had not spoken, "Well to continue after that brief break," I am here to announce that The Great One has chosen one of you, and we have come here to take him with us. We will accomplish the task and he will return to you."

"Who?" every chimed in together wondering when Starrho would get to the point.

Again, Mr. Loki stepped forward. Mr. Loki was so full of himself that he could not imagine anyone was greater than he was.

Mr. Mundy, the principal of the school wondered whether it was him, he was after all a great principal of the best school in Dora Valley.

Mr. Sodo, the chief inspector of police wondered if he was the chosen one. After all, he kept the whole Dora Valley safe and he could take on a big task.

Dr. Dang wondered whether it was he as he was a famous doctor in the Dora Valley who helped many people. Similarly, several others started wondering if they were the chosen one.

Don, the bully wondered if it was he, he was a great leader in the school and had achieved many medals.

Starrho looked closely at all of them and said, "Among you is he, he is chosen for the task!"

"Who, who?" asked the townspeople wondering why Starrho was taking so long to get to the point.

Starrho walked up to Akim and said quietly, "It is him!"

There was a strange silence. Hearts sank, and thoughts churned and groaned thinking silently, "How could a 12-year-old boy be chosen for a task as important as whatever it was?" These thoughts were of course unvoiced. The silence was deep. Don, Soki, Jo and Nok looked furious, but they did not voice their feelings reeling with envy, people wondered what was so special about Akim.

Shaan spoke first and asked, "What does that mean?"

Dendal replied, "This means Akim with come with us for this task, the rest of you can pray for his safety!"

Shaan gave a sigh of relief and said, "So good for Akim, and I can attend my beauty pageant!"

Akim looked down, feeling embarrassed and unsettled, his legs trembling and said softly, "I am not worthy of such a great task, whatever the Great One wants. I am not strong, only a small boy who is bullied. I think you made a mistake."

Don jumped in immediately and said eagerly, "Akim is a loser in Dora Valley, he is bad at games, not good at studies, a good for nothing, this is a mistake!"

"The Great One never makes mistakes," replied Starrho quietly looking very hard and disapprovingly at Don. Don suddenly looked away feeling uncomfortable. Shaan went up to Akim, touched his shoulder and said, "This is wonderful Akim, you are a hero, imagine of all the Earth, you were chosen for a great task, you will make the name of Dora Valley great!"

Shaan looked at Don as she was speaking. She wanted to spite Don because she personally disliked him, and his bullying ways, and she knew Don was constantly belittling Akim. Shaan watched Don grinding his teeth. This was the first time Shaan had spoken to Akim and he was overwhelmed, why, the great beautiful famous Shaan is speaking to little poor me! He thought. Of course, Uncle Jon and Aunt Nelly were very proud of Akim. Aunt Nelly kept beaming and Uncle Jon smiled and at the same time worried what it meant by Akim going with the Star Men.

Starrho read their thoughts and said to all, "The Great One looks inside at the heart, He does not judge from the outside, and He finds strong stuff in this boy, this boy thinks of things beyond himself. He is not about himself and this is why he was chosen. The Great One said his name is Akim. Is that right boy?"

Akim nodded his head in wonder. He was baffled and flabbergasted that The Great One knew His name. He stared at the Seven Star Men silently who gazed solemnly at him.

Then one of them Zora, the adventurous Star Man said, "Akim, you are in for a great adventure. I love adventures, and you are with us, we will protect you on this mission, so you need not fear, we are here and we will bring you back safely!"

The other Star Men agreed, "Yes, you have nothing to fear, you are with us."

Aunt Nelly was suddenly overwhelmed with the fact that aliens would take Akim away and she burst in, "We are his aunt and uncle! We can't allow Akim who is only 12 years old to go with some spacemen that we met only tonight. Who know who you are! You may be the enemy and aliens invading the Earth and you might kidnap him and we will never see Akim again, Ho no thank you gentlemen Star Men, but we cannot take the risk!"

Uncle Jon said to the Star Men, "Yes, you may be good, but we cannot allow Akim to go away like this with a big risk that we may never see him again."

Dendal, the wise Star Man stepped forward and said in a strange hushed tone:

> *"A journey must be made*
> *Or the promises will fade*
> *The prophesy must stand*

Or anarchy is at hand!"

Everyone was very still. It was clearly something beyond the words that Dendal was saying. His very words sent shivers down their spines and they heard the trees rustling. There was a note of finality suddenly and there was no turning back. Suddenly, everyone felt something important was going to happen, but if turned down, indeed, anarchy was at hand!

Starrho said mysteriously, "Faith is a step in the dark, where another Hand will show the way, but that way will become brighter as you walk on that path and that way is always rewarded along the way and in the end."

The town folk slowly started to realize the reason in Starrho's words.

It was almost as if a veil was torn and they now all saw that they were all involved in a greater plan of the galaxies beyond their little valley and beyond their selves.

Akim finally spoke up a little boldly, "I knew when I first saw the Star Men that something great was going to happen. If the Great One has chosen me to fulfill it, I should not refuse, so here I am. I chose to walk this path and go with them."

"Exactly!" said Piran pleased, he was a calm Star Man with gentle face, who always wanted peace, "This step is a choice, when choice is made it changes your life. Good boy Akim, we are proud of you for taking that step of faith in the dark, without knowing what waits."

Aim's face glowed and his eyes shone. He suddenly looked different, nobler than he had ever looked before.

"Yes, yes", agreed Ms. Rani, another woman who was a teacher. She said, "These shining men look good. I can always tell a person from their eyes."

Don kept glaring at Akim, and Mr. Loki looked furious and he kept mumbling to himself, Useless boy, up to no good, a big mistake, a big mistake!

Mrs. Loki tried to tell him timidly, "I am sure it will be okay dear!" To which Mr. Loki snapped some incoherent words to her. The Star Men watched Mr. Loki very disapprovingly.

Shirley, a kind-hearted woman in the valley said, "This has to be a good decision, the Star Men look very noble, and he is in safe hands."

Everyone agreed that the Star Men were good. Uncle and Aunt noticed a big change in Akim, he looked bolder and stronger and they said slowly and rather reluctantly, "We will let you go, dear child, our prayers are with you. Pray to see you again soon!"

Akim exclaimed gladly, "Thank you Uncle Jon and Aunt Nelly, I will be back, and I know the Star Men are good and kind, I can read it in their eyes!"

The Star Men then said together, "Now, we shall go with Akim."

"Now?" asked Uncle Jon in horror, "It is still 4:00 a.m. and not yet dawn, why would you want to start on a journey at this odd hour?"

"Time is precious," replied Starrho, "We must move in His Time, and we are The Star Men, we fly strongest and swiftest at night and we cannot fly in storms and rainy weather, so when the weather is clear, we never miss that opportunity."

Aunt Nelly said, "You make hay while the sun shines!"

"Yes, in a kind of way," said Dendal smiling; "Only here, we fly the night while the stars shine."

"Then I will pack some food for you and a small travelling bag for Akim," said Aunt Nelly. "I am also giving you a bag of caramel lollipops and a box of sausages that I will very quickly fry for you. Do finish the sausages soon, dear, share it with the Star Men!"

Grinko, a very solemn serious looking Star Man said, "Oh no, we do not eat Earth food, we cannot!"

Mr. Loki asked him a little mockingly, "Then what do you eat? Do you eat rocks and stones? Or do you eat at all?"

Grinko replied, "We take food capsules."

Mr. Loki said, "Ugh!" very rudely and Uncle Jon said to him reprimanding, "I do think we should be polite to our guests!"

Mr. Loki glared at Uncle Jon and said, "You are all fools, sending your Akim with aliens, just thank you lucky stars if you ever see him again!" Mr. Loki then marched off to his house in a fury while the others stared after him. Mrs. Loki hurried after him saying, "Oh dear, oh dear, oh dear!"

Aunt Nelly returned in a few minutes came with a big basket of food and a backpack of necessities and clothes for Akim. Uncle Jon gave some money to Akim saying he will need it for the journey and for food along the way.

"How long will this task take?" asked Aunt Nelly suddenly. This was the question that everyone was thinking about, but was afraid to ask. They were wondering whether they would not see Akim for years.

"Do not fear," replied Dendal reassuringly. "It is the time of the prophecy to be fulfilled; it will be fulfilled in its time, which will be hastened, but I cannot really tell you how long."

"Well," said Mr. Mundy, the school principal trying to sound cheery, "I'm sure it won't be long and we will have our dear Akim back again!"

With that, they said goodbyes, hugged each other and Pillho the cheerful Star Man took food bag while Akim strapped the backpack on his bag. Then the townsfolk watched in wonder as a silvery wind blew down over Akim. The silver wind showered around Akim and picked him up. Then the Star Men whisked Akim along with them on that silver current of wind and they flew up like shooting stars. As Akim rose in the air, he stared at himself in amazement; he was rising in the air with no effort at all and soon was flying. He gazed down at the others and waved wildly at all of them, and shouted, "Aunt Nelly, Uncle Jon, I'll be back!"

"Well I never!" exclaimed Aunt Nelly, blowing herself with her little Japanese fan. The townsfolk all stared in fascination watching them fly away. They kept pinching themselves wondering whether this was a strange dream. Meantime, Mr. Loki back in his house lay on his bed sulking and musing *how could they have chosen pathetic Akim!* Mrs. Loki retreated to a corner of the house, furiously knitting a sweater for Mr. Loki, her heart pacing with anxiety. She hated it when Mr. Loki got into his fits of anger. The house would be hell for a few days.

All questions were reeling in everyone's mind and that night, no one in Dora Valley went back to sleep. In fact, the following day was made an official holiday in Dora Valley as no one had slept at all!

Chapter 3
The Night Journey and Tara

Akim felt himself lifted up by a strong current, like a mighty wave in the ocean. He was flying in the silver wind and starlight of the Star Men. An exhilarating rush filled him. He was glad that Aunt Nelly had given him a warm coat because of the chilly air. "Wow," he cried out, "How exciting, I'm flyingggggg!" He stared down at Dora Valley, the lights were twinkling on and he saw the crowd of people looking up at him. He felt a twinge of sadness, wondering, *Will I be back again? Will I ever see them again?*

Starrho said calmly to Akim, "Akim, you must not worry, you are here with us, and you will return safely!"

Akim said wonderingly, "You read my thoughts again!"

Starrho said reassuringly, "Only sometimes, when we really need to hear something, not always!"

Akim agreed, "That sounds better, it would be very uncomfortable if you could read my every thought!"

Akim looked down at the teagardens they flew over, and then later they flew over forests in that dark hour before dawn. The deep thick forests smelt of trees with fruits, flowers and plants. Akim had never had been allowed to go into any forest because, of course, it was dangerous with wild animals as well as snakes.

As they flew over the forest, the Star Men slowed down looking below. There was a river shining in the moonlight along the forest.

Billho, one of the Star Man called out, "Hey! We need to land near the edge of the river where there will be a cottage there and we need to find it!"

"Yes" replied Starrho "That is where we need to land, look out for that cottage, everyone."

The Star Men had eagle eyes and it was easy for them to spot a little cottage with a golden lantern lights near the banks of the river. As they landed, Akim was surprised to see them land exactly next to the little cottage. The curtains were not drawn. Roko, the inquisitive Star Man crept up and peeped in the window.

"Oh no, Roko," called out Piran worriedly, "Don't peep! I think on Earth, it is rude to peep into windows. We will knock."

"I need to make certain there is no enemy or monster in that cottage," called out Roko cheekily and kept peeping into the window.

Akim watched Roko with fascination thinking, "These star men have natures like humans, curious, they want to know things, interesting and now I hope they are not reading my thoughts!"

In the meantime, Roko kept peering into the window. He saw a tall beautiful lady with long curly tresses of shiny black hair. She was standing and putting fresh logs into a fire. She seemed to have a mug of something steaming hot on a little wooden table. She suddenly turned around and saw Roko peeping at her through the window!

Roko was embarrassed and quickly looked down, but the pretty lady had seen him. She came to the window and fearlessly called out, "Who is there? What do you want?'

"This is the lady, she is the one the Great One showed me," said Starrho softly to the others, "The Great One told us to stay with her, and we will get further directions from her and she has to come with us too."

The lady looked at them carefully, studied their faced, and then opened the door and said, "Come on in, I know you are good kindred souls or I would have never asked you in, at this unearthly hour!"

Roko chuckled and said, "Unearthly we are indeed and thank you for inviting us in!"

Starrho said to the woman politely, "Good evening, kind lady, we are the Star Men and this is Akim. We are on a mission. The mission has right now, not been revealed to us. Ours is not to know the whole future, or it will be too much to bear, but we are on a mission to save the Earth."

The lady smiled at Starrho noting their strange silvery sheens and kind wise faces. It was as if she knew they were going to visit her.

She noted Akim looking earnestly at her and said, "Sit down. I also know that I am to accompany you on this mission. I am not sure what role I play here, but the

Great One told me it is a step-by-step journey. I know
this is a very great mission and I am glad to be part of it.
Now, rest here tonight and please do have some hot
tomato soup. I know especially the boy must be freezing
in this cold night air!"

Piran shook his head and said, "We are the Star
Men, we do not eat Earth food, but of course it will be
good for Akim."

Grinko added hurriedly because he was afraid
Earth food would be terrible tasting or poisonous for
them, "We do not take Earth food or we may fall very ill."
However, as the lady insisted, saying, "This is nourishing
delicious tomato soup, once you taste it, you will love it!"

"Well" said Dendal wisely, "I am sure no harm
can come out of it, if we don't like it, well, after the first
spoon, please forgive us if we don't drink more of it!"
The lady said graciously, "Sure, just taste and see!"
They each took a bowl of hot steaming soup and tasted
the first spoon gingerly and suspiciously, almost afraid
they would fall to the ground if they were unable to
tolerate Earth food. To their surprise and delight, they
found it delicious and said so. The lady was pleased and
said, "See, I said so!"

They sipped the soup, talking.

The lady told them, "I was waiting for you. The
Great One told me a few days ago to be prepared for your
visit, which was why I have not been able to sleep ever
since, waiting for you!"

"I thought the Great One only speaks with the Star
Men and all above the stars, not to us," said Akim
surprised.

The lady replied, "The Great One speaks to all
who will listen. However, on Earth, very few do want to

listen, but there are some of us here on Earth willing to listen. And He has a mission for you, does He not, boy, and what is your name?"

Akim nodded and said, "The mission is not yet revealed. My name is Akim."

"It is a step-by-step mission." The lady repeated, "We have provision for that task for that day. Day by day, and the next day, we get fresh strength and direction. That is the way we will succeed."

"Lady, what is your name" asked Starrho.

"Tara," she said, "Come in and rest, I have a room inside with a lot of mattresses and fresh sheets."

The little hut was warm and cozy in that cold hour. By this time, the sky was turning pink and Akim was yawning. The Star Men wanted to sleep, as they were tired after the long journey from the stars to Earth.

Tara looked at them and said suddenly, "There are complex dangers ahead," and said no further. Akim shivered suddenly feeling a little frightened when he heard that and looked at the Star Men. They did not appear frightened.

Billho picked up a hat he had found in Tara's house. It was a funny pointed hat, and he asked Tara politely "May I try it on?"

"Yes," replied Tara, 'this belongs to my brother. "He lives in a faraway city far. He comes with his family to visit me once a year."

Akim said solemnly, "You are very brave to live all alone in this cottage at the edge of the forest. In Dora Valley, we have hundreds of neighbors around us and we feel safe and also happy."

Tara said, "This is my fate, this is my lot, I cannot change it, I have no choice."

Akim looked at her, wondering what she meant. Zora the Star Man with curly hair said, "Sometimes, in the most unexpected time, a new road opens, and I hope that happens for you Tara, because somehow, it does look lonely around here, I am glad you are coming with us on this journey."

Tara nodded her head and said nothing.

Billho put on the hat on his head, looked at himself in the mirror and then said to Grinko teasingly, "This hat will look wonderful on your head, Grinko." and he put it on Grinko's head.

Grinko looked alarmed and said sharply, "No! I do not like hats, especially pointed hats, they remind me of wizards!"

"What is wrong with wizards?" demanded Akim.

Grinko answered simply, "Magic!"

"What is wrong with magic?" asked Akim mystified. He always loved a good story with magic.

Grinko answered, "Magic delves into sources from the Dark Arts given by the Prince of Darkness. It seems good and wonderful in the beginning, but slowly takes us through another pathway. Its end is always destruction."

Akim listened, not quite understanding. "Sounds a bit heavy for me," he muttered. He always thought magic was wonderful and he was not sure about this prince of darkness that they were talking about, had never heard of him and asked Grinko curiously, "Are we not performing magic by flying in the air?"

Grinko replied, "This is not magic, this is the way we are designed, these are our natural abilities. All our powers are given to us by the Great One and it is in His power that we work, but magic has its source from the Prince of Darkness."

Akim shrugged his shoulders, still wondering. He always thought it would be wonderful to have powers to fly through the air and hit up his bullies such as Don with the power of magic!

In the meantime, Billho kept joking and teasing the others because he was excited about this Earth mission. This was his very first mission on Earth. The others had come before. He has a round merry face and twinkling eyes and often loved to play a joke. They finally settled down to sleep, all except Tara, wide-awake. She tried to lie down on her couch in the little drawing room, very restless that night and kept tossing and turning.

After a few minutes, her sharp ears heard a drumming droning sound and she knew something was very wrong. That drumming sound in Tara's part of the world was the sound of enemies.

Tara did not want to wake the others up, so she ran to the window and looked out, and to her horror, she saw huge black ghastly floating creatures with roots sprouting out of them. These roots were their sharp senses, which picked up signals in the air to seek out people. They had twelve candles surrounding them. These candles gave them certain powers as they prayed to the Prince of Darkness. They were soon surrounding her cottage.

Tara cried out in horror, "Oh no, the Seekers!" The Seekers were the most ferocious messengers and destroyers of the Prince of Darkness.
Tara quickly drew the curtains, praying hard. She rushed around blowing out the lamps, so only the glow of the fire in the hearth was on.

She knew something that the black floating creatures always hated. She went to her table and picked up a golden Book, which glowed in the dim light and started reading aloud from the golden Book. As she kept reading aloud, she could hear the droning around the house.

The Star Men awoke as they too had sharp ears and immediately knew there was danger around them. By now, the Seekers were banging the windows, walls and little door. It seemed they could easily break down the door as well as the wooden walls.

The Star Men asked Tara "What are these?"

Tara told them hurriedly, "They are the Seekers; they come sometimes when they are trying to find someone. Usually, they search out for the Great One's people and try to harm them. I think they got a wind that you are around, and are looking for you. They are the Prince of Darkness messengers. The Prince of Darkness cannot see where you are, but he has messengers everywhere who are always spying on the Great One's people, and I think by now, they know you are on a very important mission!"

Just then, there was a great resounding crash! The black floating creatures had broken a window and one of the creatures floated inside the cottage to their great horror. It lunged straight for Roko and tried to drag him out of the window. The Star Men rushed forward and Starrho took out a silver sword from his clothing. It was not an ordinary sword. It shone with a strange translucent light. He waved it around and said to the others "Come on all, hold hands and sing, the power of the sword will slice the spirit of death of the hour!" They stood in a circle along with Tara and started singing a song while the

Star Men all took out silver swords from their clothing waving it in the air and singing. In the meantime, the huge black creature was trying to drag poor Roko who could not get his sword out of his clothing!

The six Star Men along with Tara began to sing a song.

> *"Surround us Oh Light*
> *Fight this Fight*
> *Protect us Great One*
> *Let this battle be won!"*

As they kept singing, their voices arose high and beautiful and after a while, the black floating creatures gave shrieks of terror and the Seeker loosened its grip on Roko, dropped him down on the ground and flew out of the window.

As the Star Men kept singing in a circle, something strange began to happen. The song rose higher in the air, and suddenly they were surrounded by light. It was not ordinary light, very bright, white, not blinding and beautiful. It had a warm feeling about it and the light shielded and hid them. The Seekers gave howls of terror on seeing the light. The banging of the door and windows and walls of the house started to lessen and then suddenly stopped!

As the creatures were flying away, Tara and the Star Men heard their yells, as they could not bear to look at that light.

With loud eerie screams, the Seekers disappeared into the night. Finally, there was silence. Everyone was relieved. Tara went to the broken window, looked out and said, "All clear, gone!"

Piran looked at the broken window and said, "I think we have to fix that window right now, just in case they try to come back."

Tara said, "I have an extra windowpane in my storeroom; I always keep extras in my storeroom because our market is so far off." "Sometimes we have terrible storms with hailstones pelting the windows. Once before, the Seekers broke my window, because they were angry with me. They know I belong to the Great One. I called out Words from my Book, and this seemed to scare them off that time!"

The others thought Tara was remarkably brave to live alone, knowing that the Seekers could come and attack her at any time.

When Tara brought windowpane, the Star Men helped to fix in the thick glass window, and it looked bright and sparkly with the new glass.

Tara said to the Star Men with an amused smile, "When you took out your silver swords, I thought you were going to kill the Seekers!"

Dendal said softly almost singing:

"Our weapons of warfare are not as of the Earth
Our weapons are powerful.
Our weapons never kill
Because violence is not the answer
for the problems on Earth.
Killing and more war begets more wickedness
The cycle of revenge will never end
Our weapons are different
But more powerful
Than the violent weapons
That humans use on Earth."

Tara agreed impressed with the song and words and nodded her head. She was suddenly very tired and yawning she said, "Yes indeed I agree, violence begets more violence and the cycle never ends and in the end, nothing! … I think I am ready to hit the sack now. I am so tired as I have not slept for a few nights, and we have a long day tomorrow!"

They are all tired, and later, sleepily the Star Men went to their mattresses and fell asleep immediately. The Star Men started to get more tired and sleepy on Earth. When they lived in the sky, they never got tired. The Earth air was different.

Zora said to Roko, "You were mighty brave when those monsters were attacking you."
Roko replied, "You all were so great and helped me, you could get them out so fast, you kicked them out with the Song. The Words of the Great One has power over the darkness."

Billho said wonderingly, "I never knew Earth was so dangerous."

Grinko said, "The humans are not as dangerous as the invisible creatures of the darkness and the poor humans can't see them so they keep fighting with each other. They do not realize that the invisible enemy is making them fight. However, they have a choice to kick them out, to take the help of the Great One, but many of them don't want to. They find it silly."

Dendal nodded his head with sadness and said, "Poor Earth people, some are wise, but the foolish are more foolish. They keep quarreling and bickering about silly things, and you know what, in the end, all that they

keep fighting about will not matter at all in the very end
of their lives and in the end of the Earth.

Starrho said, "Poor Earth people! Now, we got to
catch some sleep, we have to walk tomorrow morning as
we cannot fly in the day."

Billho asked a little impatiently, "But where are
we going, still no word from the Great One!"
Piran smiled and said gently, "In this step-by-step
journey, the doors will swing open as we walk along. Yet
at times, we may have to stand still, but even in standing
still, something great can happen if the Great One is in
that stillness."

Billho nodded, not quite understanding. He was
used to the predictability of the stars, and Earth was
chaotic for him. Still he liked it, and found the people
interesting and food quite good too. He liked Akim and
Tara, and so with a happy smile, he finally fell asleep.

Throughout all this, Akim was fast asleep,
dreaming a great dream unaware of anything.

The other Star Men looked across at Akim and
smiled at him wondering how he could be in such deep
sleep. The truth was, that night, Akim had a very strange
dream. He dreamt of a great task, sealed in a big white
packet. No one knew what it was yet and they were all
waiting for the revelation of the task. In the dream, Akim
kept asking the Great One to reveal the task. Finally, the
packet opened and a scene unfolded like a movie picture.

Akim saw a huge Golden Book, called the
Original Book of the people of the Earth also known as
the Book of Truth. The Book glowed and shone. Out of
the Book, many copies rose out and were shared with the
people of the Earth. As people read the Book, the people
on Earth grew in wisdom, kindness and love.

Then, in the dream, a long, long, green snake came and started whispering in the ears of people that the Book was not really true and that it was myth, a fairy tale, legend and that parts of it were just made up to suit people imaginations. The green snake kept whispering to the people that he would give them greater knowledge, wisdom and development. The green snake said he would share the secrets of the Universe with them. He told them that the Book would never let them develop into the magnificent humans that they were created to be. He kept whispering that he would make them gods on earth. The people like the idea of that.

Slowly, as the people kept on listening, they stopped opening the copies of the Golden Book and stopped reading it. They started reading other books, which had a lot of knowledge and made them powerful and more knowledgeable. The copies of the Golden Book gathered dust on shelves.

The number of people who read the copies of the Golden Book dwindled. Slowly over time, the Truth got diluted mixed with some lies and new teachers arose to mix the truth of the Golden Book with some lies, so people started to lose their understanding and clean hearts. Greed and want entered people's lives.

One day, the Original Golden Book disappeared! No one could find it. By now, no one thought much of the Golden Book and in fact, they all forgot about the Golden Book except for a few people who had copies of the Golden Book. Since the original Golden Book was lost, the few people who had copies of the Golden Book were struggling to obey their copies as the light had left their books.

Soon on the Earth, any mention of the Great One or the Golden Book was forbidden in public places such as schools or workplaces. People said the Golden Book was a lie given to control people's lives. People did not want that kind of control anymore. They wanted freedom.

After rejecting the Golden Book, people became more violent, intolerant. Quarreling, bitterness, hatred, revenge and wars grew on the Earth. Darkness covered The Earth. There were areas of light where good people who practiced the Book lived, but that light was also fading slowly.

In the dream, Akim heard the Great One's voice that sounded like thunder mixed with oceans of water, His voice shook the Earth and He said, "That Book has to be found and brought back to the people and the Light has to be released again. In that Light, people will get great understanding. Set the trapped Light free; find the Golden Book; make copies for all people to read, whoever is willing to read. Those who seek Truth will accept the book. I will show you gradually, how to do it, just walk along the pathway! Moreover, one more thing, help those along the way who need help. Do not turn them down!"

Akim said in a faint trembling voice, "Yes, Great One." and then after that dream, Akim fell back into a deep sleep. He slept late into the morning and when he got up, he saw a bright morning with blue, red, and green canaries singing outside the window in the forest. The Earth seemed golden that morning and Akim started to sing. Akim who never sang started singing that morning! The Star Men stared at Akim. His face was shining. They knew something new had happened to him.

Akim told them excitedly, "The Great One spoke to me last night in a dream. He showed me the mission!"

Everyone gasped. They did not tell Akim about the attack the previous night, as they were eager to hear what he had to share with them. Finally, this mission was heading somewhere and as they waited, Akim proceeded to tell them the details of the dream.

Chapter 4
The Mission Disclosed, Travel, and Ms. Grumblepot

That morning, everyone listened in wonder as Akim retold the dream, sipping cups of hot steaming tea and eating breakfast.

Tara listened intently and said thoughtfully, "Green snake, you saw a green snake in your dream? That is interesting Akim" Tara kept thinking hard and suddenly exclaimed excitedly, "I got it!"

"What?" asked everyone surprised at her excitement.

Tara replied, "People say that a green snake lives in the City of Skilk. Unfortunately, this city is beyond the Seven Seas, very far away, my dears. It will not be an easy journey, but I am sure that green snake lives there, because it is not an ordinary snake. They said it is a strange talking snake!"

Starrho said wonderingly, "That is why the Great One has called you to come with us, you know so much and have a big role to play along with Akim."

Tara smiled and said, "All of us are special in this big mission, we all have something great to do!"

Akim said excitedly, "We have to go to the City of Skilk as soon as we can, the longer we wait things will get worse." Akim suddenly seemed to have a new courage and Zora smiled at Akim, his merry eyes crinkling and sparking and said, "That's the spirit my boy, the spirit of moving forward in the plan."

Akim replied, "After that dream last night, I almost felt as if I met the Great One and sense the urgency that we have to move fast."

Tara said, "I got something to show you." She went to an old black box, pulled out a yellow tattered map. It looked a very interesting complicated map full of forest, mountains, rivers, towns, cities and seas. Tara pointed out to a city far away beyond the seas and said, "This is the City of Skilk, a huge coastal city of trade and wealth, right across the Seven Seas."

Akim looked a little disappointed and said, "This will take ages to reach!"

Tara replied, "Yes, it is a long journey. To reach the Seven Seas, we would have to go across mountains, plains and forests and eventually the Seven Seas. Again, we have to fly with the help of you Star Men, you know we cannot take an airplane as you have no passports and your very presence will raise a lot of questions with your glowing silver sheen that would attract a lot of attention."

Starrho laughed and said, "I keep forgetting that we look so different. In the daylight, we shine less."
"Well," said Dendal, "We will have to start moving after breakfast. We will start by walking as it will take many days I should think to reach, even by flying."

"I thought you did not move in the day," said Akim surprised.

Dendal said, "Since arriving on Earth, we are feeling different though we definitely feel the strongest in the night. But we can walk in the day and we will not shine as much, which is good or we will attract attention wherever we will go."

Tara replied humorously, "As I said, my dears, you still attract attention with your silvery beards and your gleaming eyes, and yes, even though it is day, we can still see a glow to your skins!"

The Star Men looked down at themselves alarmed.

"Don't worry," said Tara reassuringly, "It might help you because people will know you are different and powerful and somehow will not try to mess with you!"

"I certainly hope so," said Starrho.

After breakfast, Tara pulled out bag of gold coins, packed a heavy lunch bag and took a huge bottle of spring water. By now, the Star Men had started enjoying the taste of Earth food.

"Earth food is actually quite delicious!" said Billho smiling, "Sometimes it is better than our food capsules"

Tara said "Ah, any day better, dear Billho."

"Good news for me," said Akim "I was beginning to worry that it would only be me and Tara eating on this journey!"

Soon, Star Men, Tara and Akim set across the forest. The sheen of the Star Men dimmed a little in the day, though they still had a slight glow about them and the Star Men were secretly glad that they did not meet anyone along the way. They set out walking towards the terrain of the mountain.

They walked the whole morning and by afternoon sat down by a stream to have lunch. After lunch, the Star

Men needed their nap as they rested more in the day and were getting a little tired in the Earth atmosphere. They lay on some soft grass and went off to sleep. Tara went to sleep on soft mattress of springy moss as she had not slept properly for days. Akim was bored as he sat alone watching a little brown rabbit scuttle by him on the green grass. He started thinking about Dora Valley thinking *hope Uncle Jon and Aunt Nelly are doing good, wonder what they are doing..."*

At 4:00 p.m., Star Men got up, yawned, and Tara also sat up rubbing her eyes. Soon, they started walking again.

"We will fly in the night across the mountains," said Starrho.

"Let's get something to drink before we go," said Tara "Something sweet and refreshing!"

"Let's go," agreed the others. As they walked on, they came to the edge of the forest and saw a huge signboard. They stopped to read it, it read "Welcome to Grump Town."

"What a strange name!" exclaimed Roko, "Imagine being called "Grump Town, I bet there are grumps in the town!"

Everyone laughed. They saw a huge road after the signboard and many houses and shops scattered all over. The little lanes through the town looked crooked and the houses and shops looked crooked too.

"It should have been called Crooked Town instead of Grump Town," remarked Akim.

"Well," replied Dendal, "When a person's heart is grumpy, everything starts to become crooked!"

Akim agreed and said, "So true, we have a woman like that in Dora Valley, she is always grumbling all the time, and she cannot see anything good, even when there is good. I guess she sees everything crooked."

Grinko said, "Such a lady will need the Golden Book, hope it can help her."

Tara said, "Sure, the Golden Book is to help the sad, miserable, sick, but the only secret is, they have to receive its Truth. If they reject it, there is no hope for them. Once people accept the Truth, the Golden Light illumines those Truths to their hearts, which is the secret."

Akim said wonderingly, "Sounds interesting, I like the idea about the Golden Light."

Everyone agreed.

They were all hungry and thirsty as they kept walking down the town. As they made their way down the street, they noticed the people in the town were staring at them queerly and whispering as they were passing them.

They heard a woman whisper loudly to another woman who was standing next to her, "What strange peculiar people are coming to our town. Look at their silver beards and the eerie shine about them. Look at that tall beautiful woman, and that little boy. Are they the prisoners of those silver-looking men? Gives me the creeps, are they ghosts or aliens; should we call the police?"

"I think we have to," whispered back the other woman, "But the police can't do much to aliens or ghosts. I hope these creatures won't catch us and eat us!"

Both the women trembled almost waiting for the Star Men to gobble them up. The Star Men, Tara and Akim merely walked on by pretending they had not heard anything.

They bought cool sweet drinks from the little shop. Just then, a tiny kitten hobbled near them mewing piteously. They noticed the poor animal had a broken leg. Starrho picked up the kitten, and stroked his leg. Before the amazed eyes of the watching people in Grump Town, they saw the broken leg become straight again, healed and the kitten started playing merrily as if he had never been hurt.

"Must be a dangerous wizard with devilish powers," whispered the woman again loudly, "I never liked the looks of these strange shining creatures, they are sure to be venomous and dangerous!"

The other woman said, "Hush, they will near us, better we go fast before they attack us, they look dangerous!"

Just then, another plump woman came up spoke to them. She had frowns, wrinkles and looked extremely grumpy.

She looked at the Star Men and said, "I saw what you did, that was my kitten, his leg was broken. I was bringing him back from the vet who said my kitten would limp for the rest of his life. I must thank you for healing him, but I just don't know how you did it, you must be very gifted."

Starrho replied gallantly, "You are most welcome, lady, you are a great lady because you received the healing of your kitten without any doubt or question."

The woman laughed a little self-consciously and said, "I am not all that wonderful, I have terrible troubles and I am miserable every single day. I see you are strangers in this town. May I invite you to my house for dinner tonight? My name is Ms. Grumblepot."

Akim had to hold himself from laughing aloud for her name indeed was an unusually funny name and he thought *Now why would anyone call themselves Grumblepot beats me*!

Tara looked at Akim and smiled as if she could read his mind.

The Star Men, Tara and Akim politely agreed to come to her house for dinner, planning to fly across the mountains after dinner.

Mrs. Grumblepot kept talking as they walked to her house. She kept glancing at Tara as she found her exceptionally beautiful and kept wondering why she was with the band of strange men who looked very different yet somehow she knew they were kind.

Mrs. Grumblepot, "I had a terrible day today, I could not get up in the morning, my arthritic pains were atrocious and I could feel my joints terribly inflamed. However, I was still able to make a sumptuous dinner, so I will be happy to share it with you. May I ask, where are you from and where you going, if I do not sound too inquisitive?"

The Star Men decided they could trust Ms. Grumplepot and told her they were going towards the mountains, though they did not tell her they were the Star Men from beyond the stars as they thought it would be too much for her to swallow.

"The mountains?" enquired Ms. Grumblepot, "No one ever ventures to those mountains. They are treacherous mean mountains. They say no one can come out of the mountains alive. There are bad spirits roaming around the mountains. It is a terrible place; I think you should not go that way, if I may say so."

Dendal replied, "Thank you for warning us, but we will be safe, you know, nothing will happen to us!"

Ms. Grumplepot looked at them strangely, and said nothing further about it. She kept talking about other things. Her voice sounded like bubbling water that kept mumbling, grumbling and complaining about everything. She complained about the pot-holed roads, the snoopy neighbors (which secretly the Star Men. Tara, and Akim agreed with), and the nasty police officer down her lane who did nothing to help with the robberies in the town, and the awful town society that did nothing to improve Grump Town.

She finally brought them to a wooden cottage and said, "Here you are, welcome to my rickety cottage, everything is falling apart! That tap has been dripping for days and the silly plumber keeps making excuses and never turns up. He is just plain lazy!"

Tara said graciously, "Well, your house has a good feel about it, there are some houses that make people uncomfortable when they walk in, but yours has a comfortable feeling."

Ms. Grumblepot said, "Thank you lady, well, that is good news for me!"

As they went inside, they sat down quietly, while Ms. Grumblepot hustled and bustled around. Tara offered to help her, which Ms. Grumblepot firmly refused. Akim started wondering why they came to Ms. Grumblepot's house when they had to go on a long journey.

"We have a mission here," said Dendal quietly to Akim "I know you are wondering why we came, but there is a reason."

Akim nodded and whispered back, "I am always amazed at your uncanny way of reading thoughts!"

Finally, Mrs. Grump served dinner and as they ate a good meal of hot mashed potatoes, meat gravy, and steamed vegetables. Ms. Grumblepot grumbled on, "I am fed up and tired of this town, I wish I could just leave. It is a miserable town and the people here are frightful, all gossiping and tale bearing, sly, and pathetic. I wish I could go."

"Ms. Grumplepot, I have an answer for you," said Dendal.

Ms. Grumplepot answered sharply, "What? No one has answers for me, nothing good will ever come out of this town, and there is no answer for my pain and suffering."

Dendal looked at her, his eyes glowed in the evening light and he started to glow, as did all the other Star Men. The Star Men always glowed more in the evenings, and whenever they were speaking something important, they would start to glow more brightly. Ms. Grumblepot suddenly noticed it and gave a start. She stared at them, suddenly slightly afraid, realizing that she had strange men who glowed a little queerly, which was not natural.

"I think these are ghosts!" she thought wildly. "Oh no, I invited ghosts to my house, what a fool I am, that tall pretty woman and that boy must be ghosts too!"

Dendal spoke soothingly, "Ms. Grumblepot, we cannot heal your arthritic pain as we did your kitten because even if we healed it, the pain would come back. Yours is a different problem. It is a wound in your mind and heart. You are angry and that anger has sent signals all over your body to give you more pain. Now I want you to do something, whenever you feel like a bubbling grumble coming out of your mouth, stop it. Instead, think of something wonderful or sing a happy song. Think of happy thoughts. Don't question it, just do it."

"Well this is just baby stuff!" exclaimed Ms. Grumblepot almost angrily, "What a pseudo solution for a problem like mine. Do you think I am a fool to do such a silly thing? I am on so many medicines for my pain and a silly solution like that will never help me, never, singing a song! And anyway, I have a miserable life with no good thoughts and I don't know any songs.'

"Sometimes, it is the wisest to be like a child, for they have the treasures of life!" replied Dendal. "Do you remember any songs as a child?"

"This is ridiculous…" Ms. Grumblepot started saying, but as she felt the Star Men had some kind of power, she thought it better not to argue with them.

She opened her mouth and tried to hum a tune. She kept opening her mouth like a goldfish and closing it. No song could come out of her and she felt foolish. After a while, a little hum came out. She continued humming and as she continued, she felt calmer inside. Then she got tired of humming and stopped.

She opened her mouth about to start with another tirade of complaints but then thought better of it when she realized the Star Men were watching her keenly. She closed her mouth and opened it again, and tried to gulp down a big grumble that was coming out. Her grumbles were so much part of her that she could not stop.

Still she tried to sing again, starting softly and a little shyly, a song she remembered as a little girl,

> "Silver rain is falling
> Healing me within
> Sunrise is dawning

Joy is calling
To a brighter day
I'll follow the way"

As Ms. Grumblepot sang, she felt something rise within her, break free and she started laughing after many years. She stopped suddenly embarrassed and said, "Sorry, but I have never felt so joyous, not for a long, long time."

The others beamed in delight at this amazing transformation.

Dendal said gladly, "Ms. Grumblepot, never stop singing, keep singing, let this be the decision you make, and also keep thanking The Great One who made all things and you will see your life will change."

Mrs. Grumplepot said, "I am so amazed that such a simple solution brought me so much happiness, now I need to give you all my special yellow pudding!"

Ms. Grumblepot got up from her chair to give them her special yellow pudding, and suddenly gave a cry, and shouted, "It's gone, it's gone, it's gone!"

"What?" asked Akim, "The pudding? The pudding is gone, did someone steal it?" He was a little disappointed that the pudding was not there. He had been looking forward to it!

The Star Men knew what had happened.

Ms. Grumblepot cried out in delight, "My arthritic pain is gone! "For the first time in years, my hands have un-clawed themselves and my knees are no longer twisted!"

Everyone laughed in joy. Grumblepot stood up and made a solemn declaration, "From tomorrow, I am going to go around the town, spreading a message of no gossip, no grumbles, instead sing happy songs."

After the delicious yellow pudding, they said goodbye to a very happy Ms. Grumblepot.

Starrho told Mrs. Grumblepot ceremoniously, "From now on, you have a new name, "Ms. Joy" and you will have a new life a happy life. You will also share how your life changed with the people in Grump Town. People will start to believe what you are saying because they will see the change in you, and they will all start to change. At that time, you must declare a new name for Grump Town; it will be called Simchah Town which means joy and gladness!"

Dendal told her "The town would change for the better because of your own change!"

Ms. Joy was delighted. Her face had changed, her frown lines almost faded, and she looked younger. Something truly amazing had happened to the previous Ms. Grumblepot who was now Ms. Joy!

Chapter 5
The Mountain and the Midnight Visit

The stars started to glitter in the night sky. The Star Men made a circle and then flew off with Tara and Akim before the astonished eyes of Ms. Joy who had come out of her house to wave them good-bye. Ms. Joy stared after them in amazing and said wonderingly, "So they were angels sent to me, they are so kind and wonderful, they have to be angels. What a blessing, angels visited me today."

Meantime, the Star Men flew up in the starlit night towards the mountains, with Tara and Akim flying along under the strength of their winds. However, after flying for a while, Zora exclaimed out in dismay, "Something is wrong."

"What is it?" asked Tara worriedly.

Zora replied, "Look at the mist swirling thickly around that mountain. We can never fly through such thick mist," "We can only fly through clear nights, not cloudy or misty nights."

Starrho thought hard and said, "I vote we walk up through the mountain fog and maybe we will find a cave to wait while it will hopefully clear. What do you think?"

"Hey ho, right on, yes!" agreed everyone. They flew on until they reached the thick mist, and then it was impossible to fly further. They started to walk up the mountain. There was no mountain path. Starrho produced a hatchet and started clearing the way of thickets, underbrush, shrubs and dense grass. "Follow me," he called out.

They kept walking behind him as he kept clearing the dense bushes.

"Where is the path?" groaned Akim.

"I am the path," said Starrho, "Just follow me. It will be slow, but we will be safe."

They kept following Starrho as he kept clearing the way. As they walked upwards, the fog was dense and swirling mist surrounded them. They could hear hyenas, jackals and even the wolves howling in the distance. It was frightening. They saw brown bunnies hurrying into their burrows to hide from the hideous howling of the jackals and wolves.

Then to their delight, they suddenly they saw a light way up in the mountain.

"Let's follow the light," said Akim. "I think those wolves and jackals will not spare us if they manage to sniff us out. I hope someone kind will let us in tonight."

They finally reached closer to the light and found out that it was a tiny hut. Outside the hut, they saw a little dwarf with a round happy face, sitting near a fire, with a cooking pot hung on stilts of some delicious food over a roaring little fire. He had big soulful kind eyes. He also looked very surprised to see the glowing Star Men, Tara and Akim.

"Hi there," he called out cheerily, "It is a foggy night and the jackals and wolves have gone berserk. Do come and warm yourselves by the fire and I will share a meal with you."

Starrho replied politely that they said they had already eaten dinner, but were glad to sit with him near the warm fire.

"My name is Bojo," said the dwarf. "And if I may ask, what work do you have here?"

The Star Men decided to tell Bojo about the mission, because they felt he would be able to help them with directions and guide them. Dwarves generally had special abilities and were very knowledgeable and clever, and he looked a kind dwarf.

As they warmed themselves near the fire, Tara and Akim warming their cold toes, they talked and as Bojo heard about a little about their mission, his eyes grew wider and said, "I had a sense you were important messengers, but I had no idea you have such a mammoth task. Times are hard and we need help; I wish you all the best, we need people like you to stand in the gap!"

Akim asked Bojo curiously, "Why do you say, times are hard and what gap are you talking about?"

Bojo told them sadly, "We are living in difficult times as a hate message is spreading around all over as far as I know. The towns and valleys have spies and there are people who want to control everyone to make them do whatever they want them to. There is no love or acceptance for each other as it used to be in the old days. Hatred is on the rise, people kill people if they do not agree with the local leaders or if they think differently. I have never seen something like this before! You come as messengers to help us, which is why you stand in the gap."

Dendal said, "This is why we have come to Earth. We have to find the Green Snake."

Bojo listened to this amazed and said, "I now feel such hope. I believe you are the answer to ALL these problems. The Green Snake is the greatest evil besides of course the Prince of Darkness. In fact, the Prince of Darkness controls the Green Snake. No one can destroy the Prince of Darkness, but a time will come when he is going to be destroyed. For now, if the Green Snake is put away, things will be much better on Earth. He spreads lies and confusion to the people. He has to be found and destroyed. There will be great victory on Earth. They say he does not go anywhere, he stays in one place, but he sends out lie signals all over the Earth."

Tara said, "I have heard exactly the same thing, the Green Snake sends lie signals all over the world, it is important we find him, he is wrapped up in the whole mystery mission."

Bojo said, "I will help you as much as I can. I know the direction towards the City of Skilk; you will have to cross the Seven Seas to reach the City of Skilk. You would have to fly over the mountains towards the Seven Seas. They will be many messengers of darkness who will want to disrupt your mission, so do not trust anyone along the way.

Akim asked, "What kind of messengers, how would we know they are bad?"

Bojo replied, "We can never know what kind of form they come in. However, I think you will be warned in different ways. Be very careful, the City of Skilk has many deceptive people. Though it is a very wealthy city, strangely, there is a lot of poverty, because there is so much greed. The greedy get greedier and richer and the poor have very less. It is an unhappy city. Remember, as I said before, you cannot trust anyone in that city. Do not receive shelter from anyone. You have to find your own way around."

The others nodded, listening to Bojo intently as he told them some more stories of the mountains.

Slowly, the fire burned out and they went indoors. The Star Men started feeling sleepy because foggy misty weather always made them feel sleepy and they dozed off on the soft warm rugs that Bojo placed on the wooden floor for them.

Akim dozed off too, and suddenly got up with a start. He looked at the old grandfather clock hanging on the wall. It was 2:00 a.m. in the morning, but because it was so misty, cold and dark, the Star Men were fast asleep. They were in fact gently snoring! Something they never did beyond the stars. Earth life certainly was changing them! Tara too was fast asleep on a soft mattress in the corner.

Akim watched them sleep as he sat up on the soft rug in the corner. He was too excited to sleep after hearing all the tales that Bojo told them. Then he saw something strange. He suddenly saw a bright light shine on Grinko. A little later, he saw Grinko get up and quietly walk out of the hut. Akim was alarmed, got up and ran after him. He saw Grinko going out in the dark treacherous misty mountains.

He got up and ran after Grinko calling out "Hey Grinko! Where are you going?" Alarmed, wondering what had happened to Grinko.

Grinko swung round and said fiercely, "Ssshhhhhh, be quiet, I have to do something important tonight, The Great One told me to do it now, and I have to go."

Akim asked him surprised, "How can you go in this weather? I thought Star Men don't fly in foggy weather?"

Grinko replied, "I am going to fly south, the weather will clear in a few minutes as I fly south."

Akim asked curiously, "It is related to finding the Golden Book?"

Grinko shook his head, his silver curls glowing, and his long serious face very solemn, "No Akim, this is a different mission."

"Shouldn't we hurry to get rid of the Green Snake and get hold of the Golden Book, why are you detouring, this is not part of the mission?" asked Akim puzzled.

"I am not detouring Akim," replied Grinko gently, "Sometimes, when we are fulfilling a mission, someone on the way needs help and we must not ignore that person."

Akim looked at him wistfully and said, "Can I come and see what you are doing, Grinko? This will help me to understand what kind of things I need to do on my mission."

Grinko replied patiently, "No two missions are the same Akim. Each mission is unique and everyone's task is different, everyone's talents are different and we learn different and new things on different mission."

Akim said, "Explain, I do not understand. I feel I have a very insignificant task compared to the great things you can do"

Grinko said, "Even if a task does not look very important, it may be one of the most important tasks, so we must never underestimate anything or anyone. However, yes, Akim, you can accompany me. Come along, there may be something that you can learn from this!"

He held Akim's hand and they walked together through the swirling mist. At first, Grinko struggled in the heavy mist and Akim too found it difficult to breath in the thick fog and could hardly walk along. Akim at one point felt he would fall down to the ground. They did not give up and battled through the fog.

Grinko said, "There is an old wise saying, "When the going gets tough, the tough get going, so we have to battle through the fog!"

After 15 minutes of tough battle, the air started to clear slowly. The mist then suddenly vanished. Grinko got up and carried Akim in a powerful silver wind that picked them up and flew on southwards. The sky was bright and the sky twinkled merrily with thousands of stars.

As they kept flying over forests and fields, Grinko started to tell Akim a story:

"Akim, once there was an important minister. He had to go to a cabinet meeting held with other important dignitaries. As he was travelling in his carriage with his convoy on the highway, he saw a man lying on the road, covered with blood. The man was dying and he had a white horse next to him, dead. One of the minister's own vehicles from his convoy had hit the man.

The important minister said to himself, "Someone will see that man, pick him up and take him to the hospital. I do not have time to help him; I have to reach the important meeting on time."

With that, he ignored the man and they drove on, and finally reached the meeting on time.

The other dignitaries met the minister grim-faced to report that a carriage from a travelling convoy had hit the main dignitary, who often traveled alone on his white horse. The convoy did not help him but rode away quickly. There were many travelers on the road but no one stopped to help him! The dignitary had been lying, bleeding on the road for a long time with no help and died!

The other ministers cancelled the meeting, as the main dignitary was dead!

The minister realized in horror that his own convoy had hit that dignitary on the road and the horror was they did not help him and he died. The minister did not get his promotion, which he would have received if the dignitary had been alive!"

Akim said, "How sad!"

Grinko said, "Sometimes interruptions seem a nuisance and we do not stop and help others, but many times, those interruptions are sent to people on Earth in disguise as a test, to give them an opportunity to perform something great on Earth and help another person!"

Akim replied, "Well, I hope to always stop and help when people need it!"

Grinko said, "It is an important lesson to learn, help people along the way, this is also a part of the great mission, even though sometimes it may seem an inconvenience."

They finally came to a town where street lights were shining along the roads. Grinko and Akim kept flying over the town until they came to a house with a big garden with an apple tree growing near the house.

Chapter 6

Grinko flew down towards a window that was open. As they flew to the window, Akim gasped with amazement! They came to a bedroom where a little girl around nine years old was fast asleep. Her room glowed brightly now with the starlight and Grinko's glow, which grew brighter in the night star light.

Suddenly the girl opened her eyes sleepily and then gave a gasp. A silvery light filled her room unlike any light she had ever seen and then she saw him, a tall thin silvery man with a long serious face, and a silver beard standing at the corner of her bedroom watching her silently. She did not notice Akim because she was so fascinated with Grinko.

The girl gasped exclaiming, "Who are you?", "What do you want?"

Grinko answered her gravely. "I am a Star Man. I come from beyond the stars. The Great One wants me to show you something, come with me; we have to go on a small journey."

The girl was curious despite herself. Somehow, the presence of the Silver Man was not frightening as she noticed he had kind eyes that shone with a strange light, his face was lean and serious with a sharp nose, glistening silver curls and he had a grave but gentle face.

"What is your name O Star Man?" asked Sasha.

"My name is Grinko and the boy's name is Akim." replied Grinko.

Sasha then noticed Akim and gave a gasp and said in a surprised voice, "Hello Akim."

Akim replied, "Hello."

Sasha then turned to Grinko and said keenly, "Well, I sense something very important is going to happen, so I trust you and am coming with you."

Grinko said approvingly, "Good girl, and what is your name?"

The girl replied, "Sasha."

Akim asked Grinko, "You are traveling again?"

Grinko said, "Sometimes, when you take people out of their natural settings, they perceive things better, which is why I am taking her out."

Sasha looked at amazement at Akim and said, "Hello, you are a flying boy too?"

Akim shook his head smiling and said, "No, I can't fly. We will fly under the current of the silver wind that Grinko the Star Man will bring along with him."

Grinko raised his hand and to Sasha's amazement, told her to hold it and she would fly along with him.

Sasha shook her head, "Oh no, I will fall, I cannot fly, I am human."

Grinko explained, "As Akim explained to you, you will fly along with me in a supernatural wind that will carry you along. I will not really be holding you. Just start the first step and after that, the next step will be easier, start by holding my hand, and the rest will happen on its own!"

As the girl held his hand, they rose up and they all flew over the town. Sasha looked down, she could see tiny lights in the town glowing far below and then saw the silent countryside, and then they passed over the dense dark forests.

Grinko started flying over a plain of grasslands and then after that, she saw something shimmering in the starlight.

"It's a river!" cried out Sasha, excited, "We have come to the river!"

Grinko landed on the sands of the river. The silver sand gleamed in the cool starlight. It was a silent place and no one was around. They all landed on the powdery white sand. Grinko looked above and raised his hand.

Then something started to fly down swiftly from the stars. Sasha was stunned. What was happening! She was indeed in the middle of a very uncanny adventure! She pinched herself hard to see if she was dreaming!

Chapter 7
The Other Golden Book

To Akim and Sasha's amazement, they saw a huge Book came down from the skies. Golden light poured out of the book. Grinko whispered to Akim, "This is the Golden Book beyond the Stars; it is not the same as the Earth Golden book."

Akim was surprised that there was another Golden Book, but kept silent, watching in wonder as he saw the Book land on the white powdery sand, glowing.

Grinko opened the book and the two children gasped in amazement. It shone with writings and pictures.

The Other Golden Book

The Broad Road

Grinko gave the Book to a very surprised Sasha.

He turned the pages for her and she saw pictures, pictures of a baby. Then she saw her parents, her father and mother, both smiling, happy with the baby. As the pages turned, she saw the baby growing; it was Sasha! She saw the early days of how she made mud pies, splashed in puddles and made sandcastles on a beach. Later, as Sasha was five years old, she did some naughty things, like telling lies and not listening to her parents. As Sasha was seven years old, it showed all the events of Sasha's life, but Sasha was embarrassed, because on most days, Sasha was rude to her parents. When her parents would remind her to do things, she grew resentful and did not speak with them.

Sasha cried out embarrassed, "I did not mean to be like that, I do love my parents, please stop showing me all this!"

Grinko did not stop. "There is more, Sasha!"

He turned the pages to the chapter entitled FUTURE and as he turned, the pages showed Sasha growing into a beautiful girl. Sasha had friends who never cared if they hurt others. Sasha too became like that. She saw her mother crying and praying, and her father sad and silent in the pages. She saw herself indifferent. She did not care about them. She only spoke sweetly to them if she wanted something.
As Sasha watched these pictures, her face hung down in shame.

Sasha begged Grinko, "Stop, Grinko! Please stop, I will change, don't show me all this, I am feeling horrible."

Grinko replied kindly, "Little Sasha, it is good you are feeling pain, it means you have a conscience inside you. You still have hope. Right now, you are at the age where you clearly know right from wrong, but dear Sasha, I have to show you everything."

Grinko turned the pages.

Sasha saw a huge broad road, filled with laughing people, some well dressed, some wealthy and some poor and others miserable looking. There were all different kinds of people, but they all had one thing in common; they hated the Light and Truth and had cruel hearts.

These people did not care for anyone. Some other people in the broad road were not so wealthy, but were often resentful, angry, and revengeful. They had a motto, which said, "Never forgive, never forget, revenge is the way." Others had a motto to "kill to purify the Earth."

She then heard a Voice saying, "This is the path of destruction; all who walk this way will find eternal separation from the Great One, His messengers and Pure Ones one day when the Earth ends."

Sasha saw herself walking in the broad road. It looked easier and more exciting. She had chosen a pathway to fame and self-glorification, as she was a beautiful talented girl. She was successful in her career, and became famous. However, Sasha had one fault - she was very selfish. She had the world at her feet and all the handsome rich men proposing to her, but would often play cruel games with people's lives. She had everything money could buy, but she was not happy in her heart. She saw herself having fits of rage with no true friends, for people only liked her for what she had, not who she was.

Surprisingly, she did not see her parents in the pictures and asked Grinko where they were. Grinko looked at her keenly and said. "You were too busy to even hire someone to take care of them, and you put them in an old age home and they were sad and unhappy." Sasha cried softly, turning the pages now, and saw herself now as an old unhappy lonely woman whose marriages, (she had married several times!) always ended in disaster. Eventually, she was sick and dying and she was frightened and scared, and she had no one around her.

She saw a huge grey ugly land and she found herself walking towards it like a zombie. It was as if she could not speak or do anything, because her mind was numb. Millions of people were behind her who kept pushing her forward. She had no way out and kept walking along that line in a trance.

She did not know help was just a call away. The Great One was ever kind and wanted to help her and save her from going to that gray miserable land, but she did not understand that.

"What can I do to change this?" she pleaded with Grinko.

"There is a way," replied Grinko, "It is called Choice, a free gift the Great One has given everyone, use Choice, Sasha. We are responsible for our own life's path. We cannot blame anyone for our lives, but when we make the right choice of walking in the right path, good things will start to happen and the crooked lines in our lives will become straight again. In that path, the darkness and destruction does not have power over us to harm us."

Sasha was relieved to hear about Choice.

The Mountain Road: Grinko turned the pages and Sasha saw another path. It was a mountainous narrow pathway, so narrow that only one could walk at a time. She heard a wind howling out of the Book and a Voice said, "The ones who love the Light and Truth will choose this way though it is narrow. All who chose this path will never be separated from the Great One and will live in the beautiful Golden Land one day."

Sasha tremblingly in the picture took a step forward. She saw herself walking up the path. It first seemed difficult, but the picture had a feeling of comfort around it. Then she noticed that as she was walking, a tall golden shining person stood behind her, guiding her, and protecting her from falling off the mountain pathway.

Sasha exclaimed in delight, "The Precious One, the One who helps us on Earth!"

She saw herself later on walking with great ease on the high mountain pathway, almost skipping along. She saw herself singing with joy, and saw bursts of happiness around her, like sparkling light around her.

She then saw the mountain path again lead down to a valley, but it was a beautiful valley with green meadows and clear sparkling silver streams. She saw herself rest near the streams and drink sweet gushing spring waters nearby.

She saw other travelers like herself and as they met up, they seemed to be very kind and friendly. At the end, she saw herself along with several travelers enter the beautiful Golden Land. From the pages of the Book, she could hear beautiful sounds of singing, unearthly, unlike anything she had ever heard.

She said happily, "I want to go there, Grinko that is my choice!"

Grinko smiled at her. "Sasha, you have chosen well."

People Helped at the Last Moments

Grinko turned the pages and she saw people, walking in the broad path, but some wanted to leave and they walked out, and instead chose to walk in the narrow path in their last moments on Earth.

Sasha saw huge shining beings surrounding those people and help them up the narrow mountain path and

Sasha could hear marvelous singing coming from the Book.

People Who Turned Away

Then again, Grinko turned the page and Sasha saw people walking in the mountainous narrow path, but for some reason, they did not want to continue because they loved pleasure more and thought the narrow path was boring and so they walked out of it and chose the wide broad road instead.

"Why did they leave?" demanded Sasha.

Grinko replied sadly, "Some people never want the Truth and the Light, so they never had the Light inside their hearts that gives them the strength to overcome. These people get very discouraged when little troubles come and they turn back and leave. Those who truly listen to the Great One will always receive a glowing flame planted in their hearts. Even if they get scared or discouraged, that flame will always glow and give them great strength to overcome all their troubles.

Sasha said, "It is sad they turned away."

Grinko nodded, "In addition, some people go through a season of forgetfulness and never come out it. They forget about the wonderful things The Great One did for them. Nearly in everyone's journey, people go through the season of forgetfulness. It is by sheer will and strength that every person has to try hard to come out of it. If they do not come of the season of forgetfulness, it will eventually drag them to that gray miserable place."

Sasha shuddered when she heard this.

The Choice

Sasha said softly and quietly, "I am going on a new road forever, the narrow mountain road."

"Best choice, Sasha!" said Grinko, "And you will be strong and continue on that mountain path. You will never turn away, the Great One will help you always, and you will enter the Golden Land one day."

"Do you think anyone can ever leave the mountain path again and go back to the broad road?" asked Sasha anxiously.

Grinko said, "Sasha, once they make that choice, they will always get help to continue on the mountain path. Even if they slip or fall, or even slide back, they will get help in the right time. The Great One will help them because they truly want to do it right!

Sasha Returns Home

Sasha watched as Grinko shut the Golden Book and the Book flew once again back into the skies.

"Come Sasha, let's go back," said Grinko.

Once again, he, Sasha and invisible Akim flew up on the silver winds, rising high in the starry skies and flew over fields, forests and tiny towns, finally arriving in Sasha's own town. She landed on her own soft bed with a thud.

Then Grinko told Sasha something surprising. He said, "Sasha go and tell your parents you are coming with us, you have a part to do in a great mission that we are doing. Now that your heart is changed, you are ready for this mission."

Sasha looked astonished and said, "My parents would never let me go with strangers, I can trust you, but this is impossible."

Grinko said quietly, "Sasha, tell your parents and the doors will open."

Sasha heard the authority in Grinko's voice and hesitantly went to her parent's room and knocked on the door. Her mother was sitting up in bed, and looked very surprised to see Sasha and said, "What is it, Sasha, did you have a bad dream?"

Then she bolted in shock because behind Sasha was a tall glowing figure. By now, Sasha's father was awake and he looked very surprised to see Sasha and even more surprised to see the tall glowing figure. Then Sasha spoke and said, "Dad, mom, this Star Man Grinko awoke me and showed me my life. I have changed so much, and now he calls me to go on a mission. I don't know what it is, but I have to go."

Sasha mom said weakly, "Sasha, my child, I can't let you go with strangers just like that no matter how good they seem."

Then Grinko shining in the shadows spoke and said, "I understand your concern, but this is a mission that will save the Earth and only a few Earth people are selected in this. The Great One mentions Sasha to come on this mission along with us. She will be safe because the Great One watches over us."

Sasha's father watched Grinko very carefully and said calmly, "Let Sasha go, Mina, I sense she will be okay, and we must not stand in the way of a greater mission. Remember, this Star Man is a supernatural being, she will not be harmed."

Sasha's mother gulped and looked very unsure, but she noticed that the Star Man looked very kind and wise and finally, though reluctantly she said, "Sasha you may go, but be back soon."

Grinko said, "I assure you Sasha will be back safely and fairly soon."

Sasha's mother hurriedly packed a small bag of clothes, soap, toothpaste and brush for Sasha. Soon, before the amazed eyes of Sasha's parents, Sasha and the boy were whisked up in the air in a silver wind carried along with the Star Man. Sasha's mother began to cry when she saw that, and Sasha's father said soothingly, "I saw a great change in Sasha, she looks different, wiser, and if we stand in the way of this, Sasha will lose a great opportunity in her life. We have to let her go."

Sasha's mother nodded and calmed down though that night they did not sleep at all wondering what she was doing.

In the meantime, Sasha was having a wonderful time flying through the air, and finally, they were crossing the treacherous mountains where the thick mist had cleared.

Finally, they landed near the hut, and as they entered the little hut, they thought they would fall asleep right away, and were very surprised to find Bojo awake. Bojo was astonished to see Sasha. Grinko briefly shared their night mission. After a while, Grinko, Akim and Sasha fell fast asleep and as they slept, something dreadful happened!

Chapter 8
The Surprise Night Attack

In a faraway land near a great sea, an angry prince paced around in his tall tower. He was tall, had a sharp aquiline nose, cruel thin lips and flashing black eyes. He kept peering out of the window with a telescope from time to time. He was enraged and in a foul mood. It was past midnight.

He rang his bell connected to his magician to his tall tower. The magician stumbled out of deep slumber, rubbing his eyes, slightly annoyed to be awoken at that unearthly hour, yet afraid to say a word. The prince was a dictator. No one could dare to whisper a word against him.

The prince was pacing around the room like a caged lion, looked up and scowled when he saw his magician and snapped, "What took you so long to come!"

The magician replied, "Took me a bit of time to wake up from my sleep O Prince, sorry about that delay."

The prince snapped, "Grodo, you told me last year that someone will overthrow my kingdom. I want you to stop that person right now."

Grodo the magician was used to the unpredictability of the prince and said soothingly, "Tell me O Prince, what happened in this prediction; I am not sure I remember this prediction of mine."

The prince snarled at Grodo saying, "How could you forget your own predictions! Now let me tell you what happened. Last night, I had a dream that destruction had come upon my kingdom. This was no ordinary dream, but it was very clear and specific. The whole day this dream haunted me and now tonight I cannot sleep. I want you to find that person through your special powers and destroy that person right away, starting tonight!"

Grodo gave a grunt of dismay and quickly turned it into a cough, dismayed that the mission was murder! Grodo did not enjoy murder missions. However, to disobey the prince was out of question; if someone did not fall in line with him, he inflicted cruel tortures.

So he nodded and said, "Yes O Prince, certainly, I will find out, just give me your ten best fighters to come along with me!"

The prince growled, "The ten best fighters will be no good, I will need to send my vulture messengers. They can trace, tear and kill. They know how to find people better than anyone and they know how to fight!"

Grodo the magician nodded and said, "Fine your majesty, so be it."

The next moment, the Prince picked up an instrument that looked like a harp, played it for a moment. Soon, a cloud of black fury was flying towards the tall tower. They were black vultures, but not ordinary ones.

They were huge, had very intelligent eyes and understood every word spoken to them. They had special powers of magic, making them powerful and vicious. The head of the vultures, Kow was the only one who could speak.

The Prince said, "Kow, I want you all to fly along with Grodo, the Magician on this mission and kill."

Kow listened, bowed his head slightly and then shrieked, "Yes O Prince!" and then told the other vultures what the Prince had ordered. They all came in and stood near Grodo.

"Give me a minute," Grodo said quietly to all.

He went to a table and put his head down. He was calling upon the powers to help him to succeed to find the one appointed to destroy the kingdom.

The next moment a ball of water appeared before Grodo. It was clear, crystal, shining and as Grodo looked into the ball, it appeared he could see strange figures and images. He kept staring in the water ball and seeing mysteries.

After many minutes, Grodo looked up and said mysteriously, "Someone is travelling, something is moving, but they are far away now."

"They?" shouted the prince furious. "You mean there is more than one? Find them out and destroy them tonight!"

"Yes, O Prince, more than one." Grodo nodded.

He realized it was pointless to argue with the prince about how far the destroyers actually were now. It would be impossible to destroy them that night. From the water ball images and distance calculated, it appeared they were very far away.

Grodo said almost gloomily to the prince, "I will change and be back in a while."

Grodo then slipped on a golden robe with tiny wings. That robe enabled him to fly and he did so easily and then came back to the Prince's room, and called Kow and the other vultures to follow him. He and the vultures flew through the black sky. It was extremely dark, cold and cloudy as they flew. The Prince watched them fly away with satisfaction.

Grodo gave the vultures directions to fly. It seemed the destroyers of the kingdom were somewhere in the east. Grodo suddenly realized it was a hopeless situation and they were too far away. Grodo could not pick up their signals clearly.

They flew over the sea faster than eagles with the powers they had. After a long time, they finally reached the shores of the sea. It was dawn and the sky turned a pale pearly gray. The clouds hid the sun.

Grodo told the vultures "Now, land on the shore."

As they landed on the seashore, Grodo again sat near a rock, putting his head down and concentrating and mumbling to himself.

Kow watched him silently. His cold black hard eyes viewed everything almost with scorn and hatred. Grodo himself was aware of how dangerous all the vultures were. They could destroy anyone ferociously if they felt they were an enemy. Grodo knew that they could even turn against him if they took a sudden dislike to him. Their sharp claws could rip someone apart and their beaks could peck out flesh very easily.

Just then, an old angler got out of his boat, walking on the sand. Kow, the head vulture stared at him; he did not like the look of him. The old man had kind eyes. Vultures hated kindness considering it weakness whether in people or animals. Anything weak to them was a thing of disgust and repulsion.

Kow shrieked to the other vultures to attack the old man. As the angler continued walking on the shore, the vultures closed around him and the poor old angler began to be alarmed.

Grodo suddenly lifted his head up and saw the vultures closing around the angler.

Grodo called out to Kow, "Kow, tell them to leave him alone, let him go on his way."

The vultures did not seem to hear him. Grodo felt uncomfortable. He did not like unnecessary killing and the vultures killed anyone they disliked

Grodo softly called out and hummed a tune:

> "Do not kill today
> Do not kill this way!"

It was a strange short tune, but it seemed to have a magical effect, the spirit of killing left the vultures. The vultures flew away from the man and perched on the rocks, watching the old angler who hurried across the beach to the seaside town.

Very soon, the silver doves who lived near the sea heard about the huge black vultures. They anxiously flew through the seaside town, warning everyone about the vultures and magician. Everyone in the seaside town was warned to stay indoors that day. The angler was also busy warning everyone.

Grodo told Kow, "We need to move out of here fast, just let's get some food from the seaside stall."
The seaside stall man had just heard about the vultures, was about to close his stall and run away when at that

moment Grodo spotted him, and came towards his stall. The stall man trembled, muttering to himself.

Grodo came up and said almost rudely, "Fish, lots of it, a bag!"

The cook at the seaside stall handed a big bag of fried fish to him, white as a sheet, shivering in fear, terrified that the magician would cast a magic spell on him. Grodo did look overpowering in his golden robe and little wings.

Later, Grodo and the vultures walked down the town looking for some fresh water, but to their annoyance, found all the shops shut.

In the meantime, some children were peeping out of their cottage windows near the seaside town and giggling hard when they saw Grodo.

In one of the cottages, a boy said to his friend who was at his house, "Did you ever see such a strange sight? There is a funny strange looking man with a golden cloak and golden wings and those ugly big black birds flying around him, funny enough to be made into a comic strip!"

"Hush!" snapped his mother sharply, afraid that the magician could hear him and supernaturally enter their house. "Be wise and silent, do not utter a word or that magician will come into our house along with his band of black birds and kill us!"

Finally, Grodo spotted a tap and because he was so thirsty, drank the tap water and gave the ravens the same water. Finally, Grodo and the vultures flew away.

Everyone in the seaside town was relieved to see them go and came flooding out of their houses. Soon, beach was once again full of people and stalls. They kept exclaiming, "Good thing the wicked magician with his band of birds left so quickly."

When Grodo and the vultures set out again, Grodo told the vultures, "We need to move towards the Wild Forests. The Wild Forests are very dangerous. Bad spirits lurk there. Many a man has been killed there and also there are a lot of savage wild animals, so we need to fly a little higher, but my sensors are leading me there!"

Kow shrieked back that he agreed. Then they started fly towards the Wild Forests.

It was midnight when they reached the Wild Forests. It was pitch black and as Grodo said, it appeared ghostly apparitions were floating around in the Wild Forest!

Grodo and the vultures flew high above the forest trees in order to avoid the ubiquitous apparitions. This was not the same forest near Tara's cottage, but this was more towards the treacherous mountains.

After a long time, they reached the edge of the forest, and in the distance, they saw the treacherous mountains looming ahead. Grodo looked up and stared at the mountains, and then his very sharp eyes noticed a tiny light somewhere high up on the mountains.

"AHA!" Grodo shouted loudly and triumphantly. "There! My sensors feel it strongly there! Come on; let us fly up those mountains. Those destroyers of our city are definitely there. Now, we fly up and attack, destroy that house they are living in!"

Kow was excited and pleased to hear this and the other vultures nodded in agreement. They always enjoyed the kill. They all flew up hurriedly to the treacherous mountains.

In the meantime, Bojo, the dwarf was awake in the cottage. He could not sleep that night after Grinko, Akim and Sasha had returned. He suddenly heard a strange droning sound and ran to the window. As he peered outside, to his horror he saw black vultures surrounding the hut and a powerful looking man who looked like a magician. The magician was standing near the cottage and muttering something eerily.

The Star Men soon awoke, Tara awoke, and Akim too awoke, and immediately knew there was danger around them. By now, the black vultures were banging the windows, walls and hammering down the little wooden door and it seemed they would break down the door.

The Star Men thought of the attack in Tara's cottage, this was very similar.

Starrho shouted, "Everyone, take out your swords!" and to the amazement of Bojo and Akim, the Star Men drew out silver swords.

Akim and Bojo were wondering whether the Star Men would kill the vultures and the strange magician outside, but they did nothing like that. Instead, they started to wave their silver swords in the air.

"Come on all," called Starrho, "Hold hands and sing," They stood in a circle along with Bojo and Akim started singing a song again. As they sang, their voices rose high in the night, the ground almost seemed to shake. They sang:

> *"Surround us Oh Light*
> *Fight this Fight*
> *Protect us Great One*
> *Let this battle be won!"*

As they kept singing, their voices rose up in the air powerful and beautiful. The song seemed to infuriate the vultures and Grodo and the banging of the door became more furious.

Suddenly, everyone in Bojo's cottage heard a resounding crash, and to the horror of everyone, the door broke down and the huge vultures rushed in along with Grodo!

Starrho called out in the calm voice to the Star Men, Akim and Bojo, "Do not stop singing and Star Men keep waving your swords!"

One of the vultures swooped down and started to attack poor Akim and the Star Men rushed towards Akim waving their silver swords furiously. As the Star Men waved their swords, it sliced through the air. It did not cut the vultures or anyone, but a strange phenomenon happened. Circles of fire swirled in the air! The circles of fire then began to get bigger and started to build a wall around Tara Akim, Sasha (who had woken up, still rubbing her eyes sleepily) Bojo and the Star Men.

Grodo and his vultures rushed around the all the people and Star Men, but they could not go beyond the wall of fire. Then, Grodo and the vultures heard a strange musical sound that filled them with fear.

Grodo was horrified. His magic always penetrated anything and destroyed it. This firewall was a mystery and made him feel a little afraid. He realized he was up against a higher power than he thought. On seeing this wall of fire, Kow backed away suddenly to the surprise of everyone and began to move out of the cottage.

This was not an ordinary fire, it had the power to protect and it was sent from the Great One.

The Star Men, Tara, Akim, Sasha and Bojo saw the magician and the vultures flying away in a hurry. Suddenly, there was a deadly silence. Everyone stared at the broken door and Bojo tried to sound cheerful though he was shaking.

He said, "Hey guys, I have some plywood and nails and hammer, I can fix the door right now. It looks like an ugly gaping hole with the whistling wind rushing inside, not such a good feeling!"

Bojo tried to be cheerful as he fixed the doors and the others helped him as well.

In the meantime, as Grodo and the vultures flew back over the Wild Forests, Grodo said to the vultures, "Indeed, those people are on a mission to destroy our kingdom. They are definitely more powerful than we are! I need to call on higher magic, but not tonight, we will need to go back home and plan another attack with higher magic!"

The vultures agreed. They felt clammy and cold when they heard that eerie sound coming from the strange shining creatures. The singing of the Star Men had a greater power than Grodo's magic, which was bad news to them.

Grodo said grimly, "Definitely, these mountain people have more power and are very dangerous."

They were soon flying over the sea all the way back to their kingdom with a sense of a failed mission. They were all a little afraid to come back to the kingdom having failed the mission, afraid of the Prince's fire and fury.

Grodo kept frowning as they flew back wondering how he would conjure up fresh magic strong enough to defeat the terrible power that the mountain people had.

They arrived back in the palace in a few days. When they arrived, the prince was wide-awake, waiting. He had insomnia since his nightmare days ago.

When he saw Grodo and the vultures flying back, he was relieved and thought, "Mission accomplished, enemies killed."

He had full faith in Grodo who was a great magician. However, when Grodo told him that the mission had to be on hold for a while as these strange people had stronger magic, the prince had a raging fit, yelled and hollowed waking up half the palace.

He screamed hysterically, "You rusty idiots, nincompoops, washed out sea-water fish, fools and failures. Do something right now and get rid of those people or I will throw you to the sharks!" Everyone in the palace was now awake and alarmed.

Grodo was used to the prince's temper said soothingly, "O Prince, it is not yours to worry, I will find a way to destroy them all. I will just need a few days to get it done. Please rest O Prince, have no fear, I am here!"

Grodo's calm strong voice was balm to the frayed nerves of the prince although he was still in a fit.

Grodo went to a cabinet and took out a glass, swirled in some strange herbs to calm him down and said, "Drink, O Prince, and sleep peacefully. Tomorrow morning, I will work on a new plan and we will finish them off."

Finally, the prince fell asleep while the tired Grodo and vultures went to sleep that night after that long journey over the seas.

Chapter 9
The Day Indoors and the Seekers

The next morning back in the treacherous mountains, everyone got up late. "Good morning everyone!" called out Bojo, cheerily. "I'm glad you could sleep a bit after that nasty attack last night. Get up, and have a wash in the spring water outside, nothing like fresh spring water to wake you up!"

Tara looked at Sasha and said, "Welcome dear, we are all on a mission together, isn't it marvelous!"

Sasha said shyly, "Looking at all of you, I just feel so happy to come along on the mission though I am not sure what I have to do. I was so surprised to see the way the Star Men drove off those birds and that magician with their fire and swords…and they did not hurt anyone."

Tara said, "This is how this great battle is fought, without wounding anyone, no bloodshed, but in the end, we will win!"

Akim said, "It's hard to imagine winning a war without bloodshed, but I am beginning to realize it is possible, the Star Men and the Great One has a greater power that fights the darkness."

Everyone washed their faces in the spring water, and indeed felt refreshed. Bojo then gave them a sumptuous breakfast.

After breakfast, Bojo told them gravely, "I just got some bad news. My friend, the silver dove came over a few minutes back and told me that the Seekers are looking for you. For some reason, they are not attacking but are sitting on the trees and watching the cottage.

As the Star Men looked out, they did see the ghoulish black apparitions of the Seekers with candles glowing on their tentacles, perched on the tall forest trees waiting for them to come out.

Sasha gave a gasp of horror when she saw them and Akim exclaimed, "They like look vicious monsters!"

Tara remarked, "This is the first time I have seen the Seekers in the morning, they really are after us, and for some reason they are not attacking the hut, I think they are aware that the Star Men have greater powers."

Akim said. "Strange things happen in this part of the Earth, Bojo, why do you choose to live all alone on these perilous mountains with the Wild Forest at the foot of the mountains? Fortunately, when we came towards the mountain, we did not cross the Wild Forests."

Bojo replied, "This was my great-grandfather's home and in those days, things were not as bad as now. I was born here and then my parents died some years back. Somehow I find it hard to leave my family home!"

Akim replied, "I know one's own home is precious. However, it is just a house Bojo, a house will come and go, but you need to live in a place where you have good people and friends around you and you are safe. I think of Dora Valley where we are all so happy together. We care for each other, stand up for each other and this makes our days happier!"

Bojo shook his head and said nothing further. It appeared that Bojo was not ready to hear of leaving his family home.

Starrho said, "I think we will stay here the entire day and will fly in the evening. It will be a clear night with stars out so we can fly fast and the Seekers will not be able to keep up with us!"

Bojo nodded and said, "I thought of the same thing. You can reach the edge of the Seven Seas at night. I have very good friends who live in an island at the start of the Seven Seas, the Island of Tipukut. There is a great king ruling there. His name is King Asa and he can help you a lot. I told my dove messenger to go and tell him about your coming."

Everyone was glad that Bojo had planned everything so smoothly and told him so. Bojo beamed in delight. He was so happy that they all were pleased with him and was sad they were going though.

After breakfast, they sat around, waiting. It was a long wait and Akim was anxious and worried. Billho tried to make everyone laugh by telling a few jokes and Bojo set out to cook a cheery meal while Roko kept peering out of the window to see what the Seekers were doing. They sat on the forest trees, watching, waiting and never moving. As Akim looked at them, he shuddered.

Starrho watched Akim's anxiety and said softly to Akim, "Akim, our warfare is not of this world, it is different, it is not violent, not killing, not hatred, but our warfare is more powerful and in the end, we will win!"

Akim nodded not quite understanding. He thought the Star Men were always calm and peaceful in all circumstances. Akim wondered why such a noble task was entrusted on him when he felt so weak inside.

"I am not of noble material," he said suddenly sadly and wistfully speaking almost to himself. Dendal came and stood beside him and gently said, "Akim, I want you to remember something always, A little star can light up the dark to make that difference with a shot of faith in the dark!"

"What exactly does this mean Dendal?" asked Akim curiously.

Dendal replied, "You can make that difference on the Earth. Little stars all have a role to play on Earth and when they all shine, they make that big difference in the Earth. No task is smaller or greater, everything is important, even though it may not seem very significant to others. People on Earth only look at the big stars and almost worship them. The million little stars that light up the dark make the difference on Earth. You Akim are that little star who is going to make a great difference on Earth with your shot of faith. You agreed to come with us, and that was your shot of faith, you could have said no!"

When Akim heard those words, he felt a sudden ray of hope. People who felt small and insignificant could actually have a very important role on Earth!

Akim suddenly felt very special and precious to the Great One, chosen for a personal mission that no one else was chosen for.

Akim started singing, "I believe, I believe, I believe in the Great One." He then did a little dance and the Star Man danced with him in joy. Tara started laughing with joy and Sasha kept smiling. High above, the Great One and the Ones who lived above did a dance too. There is great jubilation that day and a dank dark gloomy day became alive with an internal truth that dawned on Akim.

Later in the afternoon, it was raining and cold, but Akim felt as warm as toast. He experienced the Great One's love and all fear left Akim. The fear of the future, the fear of the magician and black vultures, the ghostly Seekers, the fear of death, and the fear of life left Akim in an instant and Akim felt like a new boy inside.

Towards the evening, the rain cleared completely and little stars started to light up the inky blue skies. Zora said gladly, "Finally, our wonderful starry sky. There is nothing like a starry night to make us fly up high, hurrah!

"Hurrah!" echoed everyone their spirits lifting.

Bojo had prepared a merry fire indoors, Tara who was a great cook made a delicious meal, and Bojo said, "This is the best meal I've had in a long time!" to which everyone agreed.

Soon, they set out of the cottage; they could still see the Seekers sitting menacingly on the trees. Sasha looked at them nervously and Akim said, "Don't worry, they can't harm us, we have stronger powers!"

Sasha replied, "Yes, I have seen that, but still they look so menacing with those strange tentacles and candles all around them.

Grinko said, "Don't worry about them, and don't even look at them."

Dendal said to Bojo, "I hope you will be safe when we leave, I am worried about you."

Bojo replied bravely, "I'll be fine, don't worry about me!"

As they stood outside, Starrho looked at the others and said, "Let's make a circle, hold hands and sing,"

Bojo said smiling, "This is your secret that gives you your power!"

As they made a circle outside the cottage and held hands and started to sing:

"We will soon overcome
All this darkness in our way
As we walk in the Light
We will win this fight!"

Suddenly a light surrounded them and the Seekers could not bear the dazzling light. They flew out in a flurry and hurry to get away from the Star Men and their light.

The Star Men called down the wings of the silver winds and Tara, Sasha and Akim went along with them on the winds of the silver winds. As they flew up high in the sky, the Seekers had lost all trace of them. They went hunting after them but could not find them. They finally came back to Bojo's cottage the next dawn and they found no one. Fortunately, Bojo was not there.

As soon as the Star Men and the others has flown off, Bojo's cousin, Holo who lived in the valley had heard about the visit of the Star Men and Akim through the silver dove. They all feared trouble was on the way for Bojo.

Immediately, Holo along with some other dwarves came up the mountain and insisted that Bojo leave the mountain and live with him. In fact, Holo told Bojo not to go back to the mountain.

"Bojo," he said solemnly, "You can stay with me, I will be very happy to have you stay with me. The mountains are lonely and dangerous and now that the Seekers know where you live, they will come back to kill you. They will not leave you alone now since they know you are friends with the Star Men, Akim and the others."

Bojo nodded his head and for the first time agreed to leave his precious cottage, something he would have never thought of before. Times had indeed changed so much. There were robbers, killers and wrathful people lurking around. Nasty mean spirits roamed through the forests below and savage animals started trying to attack his cottage, which was why he lit a big fire every single night.

Bojo himself had never crossed the Wild Forests but had to go all around the mountains in order to reach the valley below to buy his monthly provisions.

Something else had changed over the last years as he had earlier mentioned to the Star Men and Akim. There were vicious elements roaming over the towns and mountains, maybe spies, and a message of hatred spreading over the valleys and plains. Bojo for the first time felt he needed to live closer to people he knew and loved and who cared for him.

Bojo and Holo along with a group of other dwarves emptied out Bojo's little cottage and they set forth to Holo's cottage in the valley.

In the meantime, the Star Men and Akim flew over the mountain and far, far away that starry night. The Seekers were still looking for them again, but could not find a trace of them. By early dawn, the Seekers went back to Bojo's cottage in a fury to attack Bojo but could not find him! Furious they flew around the mountain, unaware that the Star Men, Tara, Akim and Sasha had gone very far away!

And it was a good thing that Bojo had emptied out his cottage and went to stay with his cousin Holo, or definitely, he would not have survived that early dawn when the Seekers came back looking for him!

Chapter 10
King Asa, the Ship, and the Storm

Meeting King Asa

The Star Men and Akim flew a long time, travelling over forests, rivers, and valleys. As they were nearing the sea, the sea breeze blew gently on them and salty sea water sprayed on their hot faces cooling them.

Suddenly, a huge white dove flew towards them. It was not an ordinary dove as doves are never awake in the night, and he was awake at that late hour. The dove stopped before them and beckoned them to follow him, which they did.

Roko remarked, "Strange dove, it almost looks as if it can speak but does not."

Sasha remarked uneasily, "Do you think it is safe we are following the dove, supposing it's a trap?"

Tara replied, "It is possible, but as Bojo mentioned, he has dove friends, so this must be his friend."

As they followed the white dove, he led them to an island of coconuts and palm trees, forests and a little town, dotted with houses all over. Finally, he led them towards a large grand grey stone palace and as they landed on the palace grounds, a group of people seemed to be waiting for them.

A tall thin man with kind eyes and sandy brown hair with a little cap, holding a silver bell introduced himself as the Crier.

"Good evening, nice to meet you all, we were waiting for you. Bojo the dwarf told us you would be coming!" He said, "I am Crier of the Island of Tipukut. You might wonder what a Crier is, well, I cry out loud each morning from an old copy of the Golden Book to tell people the truth so they would not walk in a lie"

Akim asked in deep interest, "So you also have the golden book copy, I thought it was totally gone from the Earth, and what is the lie?"

The Crier explained, "The lie is that which not the truth is. In the beginning, the lie looks better than truth, good, and a lot of fun and success, but the end, the lie brings destruction and harm. The truth purifies and transforms people's minds to think away from the twisted lie."

Tara nodded and said, "Interesting, I think you will have to keep calling out the truth until the recovery of the original Golden Book, the Golden Light automatically help people understand the Truth from the Golden Book!"

The Crier said, "Yes, dear lady, that is so true!"

The Star Men greeted the Crier saying, "It is nice to meet you, you are doing a powerful thing for the Island of Tipukut."

The Crier said, "Pleased to meet you all!"

Starrho said, "I am Starrho, this is Akim, Tara, Sasha, and the Star Men are Dendal, Zora, Billho, Grinko, Piran, and Roko."

The Crier smiled warmly and said, "Come and join us for a feast under the stars."

Akim and the Star Men gladly sat at a huge round glistening wooden table filled with delicacies and fresh juicy fruits, and tucked in to the delicious feast set before them.

Other island folks smiled warmly at the Star Men and Akim and greeted them at the table.

"Start your feast, the King will arrive late." The Crier said. "He already has had his dinner so he ordered this for you. He told us to continue as he has some urgent work."

All sat at the round table and the Crier began to share many things with them.

"I must tell you that as you cross the Seven Seas, you will have to pass through the Island of Darkness, you cannot avoid it. If you do not go to the Island of Darkness, a thick gray mist that surrounds the island will swallow you up. You have to go there, to overcome the darkness and come out victorious.

"The Light has to always overcome the Darkness," said Tara.

"How is that so?" asked Akim in wonder thinking *is it the Light in the Golden Book?*

The Crier replied, "It is a black island shrouded in darkness surrounded by a thick mist. The inhabitants are always stumbling along, falling down, and fighting all the time. They are like parrots; they listen to whatever the leader tells them even if it is bad, because they cannot discern good from bad, someone has to help them out of this. Now when we go there, you have to show them the Truth, you will find out how to do it."

Sasha said sadly, "Must be a living nightmare there!"

The Crier agreed and said, "Yes, and on top of that, they cannot see much round them, it is always very cold and dark all the time. Their ruler is the one who flies in the air and controls the Earth. He does not live there, but lives in the air. His name is the Prince of Darkness. He travels everywhere, all over the Earth, with the speed as fast as lightning."

"Then he must be listening to us now and he must know we are going to the Island of Darkness!" said Akim looking around him.

The Crier replied, "He is not present everywhere, but he has his workers who live all over the Earth and inform him of everything happening around." the Crier replied. 'The Prince of Darkness always ensures that the island is in a terrible fog, so the people will never see the light of day and he never lets anyone pass the Seven Seas peacefully, which is why you must destroy his control over the Island of Darkness."

"How do you know all this, Crier, when you never leave the Island of Tipukut?" asked the people in the island surprised.

The Crier said, "The Great One tells me many things and even takes me to places!"

Everyone gasped in amazement. They had no idea about this.

Piran, the Star Men then said a little worriedly "We cannot fly through thick fog and mist, we are the Star Men and we fly best in star light!"

Just at that moment, a young king walked towards them. He was dressed in fine silks and wore a crown. He had a kind face, and he smiled at them warmly. He had heard what the Crier was saying about going to the Island of Darkness.

"Good evening, I am King Asa.' he said, "Your friend, Bojo, sent a message to me through the silver dove and told me all about you and I had sent my white dove to bring you here!

Everyone stood up at the entry of King Asa, but he told them, "Please sit down. Well, I think we should go along with you and also a team of volunteers to the Island of Darkness, and Crier, you have to come with us."

"No King Asa, I beg to decline," replied the Crier, "The people in the island are vulnerable sometimes. I cannot leave them alone now; they still are not strong enough to be left alone as sometimes the Seekers may come to attack."

"We experienced the attack of the Seekers too, but of course with the songs of the Star Men, we won!" said Akim said.

King Asa and the others exclaimed in horror, "The Seekers! If you have faced the Seekers and come through, you can face anything!"

King Asa added, "The power of song from the Great One has great power to defeat the enemy, though to others, it seems a weak ineffective method of war!"

"Remember," continued the Crier wisely to the Star Men and Akim, "You cannot overcome the darkness and even rescue people who do not want to be rescued or helped. Such people are beyond help. People have to want help, only then it works. I understand that they are not aware of the darkness they are in."

Everyone nodded gravely.

"Thank you for coming along with us, King Asa and all the rest of the team," said the Starrho gratefully,

"We could have flown to the Island of Darkness but we do not fly well in thick fog and mist, so your help is greatly welcome!"

Journey on Seas
A crew of a dozen people of people from the Island of Tipukut agreed to join the trip to the Island of Darkness, as it was not safe to go alone. A boy called Bravo was among them.

Bravo, the boy from the Island of Tipukut said, "Hi Akim, I am glad to meet another boy on an adventure."

Akim was happy to meet Bravo for after a long time, he found another boy of his age and the two boys became good friends.

The team left early on Sunday morning when the deep pinkish sun arose and they arrived at the shores of the Zorran Sea. They boarded a grand ship called Galleon whose captain was Captain Soto. They were given a huge supply of food, provisions, clothes, blankets and many other important things needed at sea, but they really had no idea what to do when they arrived at the Island of Darkness.

The Crier told them, "What you are doing is a step in the dark. You have to take the first step. Unless you take that first step, nothing will happen and then step by step, you will be shown what to do."

They boarded the ship, sang songs, ate an early morning breakfast and drank cups of refreshing tea.

It was a golden morning, silverfish darted across the seas, and dolphins jumped out of the sea, playing. During that long peaceful day, the crew stayed at the deck talking quietly and enjoying the sea spray. At one time, a playful inquisitive dolphin came around the ship and kept somersaulting around the ship. As the day drew to night, twinkling stars arose in the dark blue skies.

Then, all of a sudden, there was a sudden chill of air, and they shivered. Tara, Sasha, Akim, Bravo went down their cabins and settled to sleep on their cozy bunk beds, looking out of the round thick windows at the dark sea. They covered themselves with their soft blankets and sank into deep sleep. The Star Men stayed on the deck enjoying the star-studded sky.

A few days rolled by happily. Captain Soto was following a map and a compass in the direction of the Island of Darkness and they were moving in the right direction.

The Storm

One night, Captain Soto was at the steering wheel when he heard rumbling thunder and a cold draft that set his hair to stand on one end.

He muttered to himself, "This is not a good sign, such a cold draft…oh no, I think it's beginning to rain!" and he called out, "Yo ho sailors, hands on deck, there is a sudden weather change. It's rain folks, but let's hope for the best that it will be a light rain."

"Aye Aye Captain," shouted the sailors over the roar of thunder that started bellowing in the sky.

Just then, out of nowhere it seemed, a huge ugly black rat with menacing teeth ran out on the deck glaring at everyone on deck with its red eyes.

Captain Soto saw it and shouted, "Catch that scallywag and throw it off into the sea. Rats bites can be fatal!"

However, as fast as the rat appeared, it disappeared and soon everyone forgot about it as the thunder rolled in the skies and lightning cracked the black skies in half.

As the crew waited anxiously, the sea started to toss up huge gigantic waves with blue-white lightning flashed and then the pelting rain lashed out at everyone.

Captain Soto instructed sailors to keep one huge raft ready on deck, as they may need it anytime. Everyone was dismayed to hear this.

"Are we going to sink?" asked Sasha tremblingly.

Starrho replied reassuringly, "We will be fine, we have a mission to finish, remember, don't worry!"

Captain Soto shouted, "Go down King Asa, Akim, Tara, Sasha, Bravo, Star Men, go to your cabins, just be aware of that scallywag rat; rats have terribly sharp teeth!"

All ran inside except for Captain Soto, the sailors at the helm, King Asa, who refused to go down, and a few others from King Asa's team.

Akim sat on his bunk, looking out through the round window near his bunk bed while Bravo on his bunk also started out at the sea through his window. Bravo was used to the sea, but Sasha had never seen a sea storm before, neither had Akim, but he was fascinated with the huge waves thinking *Wow, I bet no one in Dora Valley ever saw such a magnificent storm*!

Akim saw Sasha looking a little nervous and said, "Cheer up Sasha, this storm will pass!"

Just as he said that, a huge giant wave shook the ship violently and suddenly, the ship was flung across some rocks by a gigantic wave. They heard a terrible groaning. The ship seemed to have hit a huge rock!

"The ship crashed, it will sink soon!" shouted Captain Soto, "Climb on the raft, go fast, jump from the ship."

Some sailors lowered one huge raft and managed to jump down lightly, helping the others climb down on the raft, tying everyone quickly to the pole in the middle of the raft.

With sinking hearts, they left their grand ship and watched it sinking slowly. They clung on dearly to their wooden raft that went sailing into an unknown darkness. By now, the waves had become less fierce and slightly calmed down by now.

It was too difficult to steer their raft in the raging storm. King Asa and Captain Soto instructed everyone to grip on tightly to the big pole in the center of the raft.

Captain Soto said, "This raft is made especially for bad storms, so just hold tight to the pole, and the ropes are holding you too, so don't worry."

"Are we going to the Island of Darkness unprepared? Asked Bravo. "I mean, we have nothing with us."

"Do not fear," replied Starrho, "It will all be alright, something will work out."

They all nodded in agreement and started singing songs. All the fear started to leave their hearts. Suddenly, the sea was calmer. Soon, they saw the trace of a gold dawn.

"Yae!" cried Bravo, "Morning has broken!"

Then another marvelous thing happened. They saw a patch of land about a mile ahead and they all gushed, "Land Ho!" and they paddling furiously toward it with their oars.

"This is certainly not the Island of Darkness," remarked Starrho, "It looks beautiful with bright flowers, fruit trees and shady trees and green grass all over."

Chapter 11
The Enchanted Island

They reached the island, and it was usually silent and still. They could find no inhabitants, but strangely, they saw a huge house. Around the house were many, many fruit trees. They noticed one particular tree with juicy sweet-smelling large pears. The Star Men had never seen such juicy luscious fruit before and Piran said, "This looks wonderful and had a sweet juicy aroma, what a treat, never seen fruit like this in the stars, this is why Earth is the most different planet!"

The crew hungrily made their way to the pear tree to pick them off, as they were hungry after the terrible shipwreck. Just when Bravo had plucked off a juicy pear, someone shouted, "Stop! No!" They turned around to see a dwarf hurrying up to them looking very worried. He had sad and lonely eyes and the crew decided he was harmless.

"Sorry for picking your pears without asking," said King Asa apologetically, "We are shipwrecked and are just so hungry."

"It's not that," replied the dwarf, "These are magic pears, if you eat them, you will come under a spell. It is a terrible spell. I am so sad that all my nineteen friends are under a spell."

"What is the spell? And what is your name?" asked Starrho?

"Dodo," replied the dwarf.

"Nice name, I mean for a dwarf!" said Akim.

Dodo smiled and said, "This Island is called The Enchanted Island. A wicked witch once ruled it. She used incantations and spells to control things and make things happen, as she wanted. We heard about that and came to destroy her power because she was doing a lot of damage to the surrounding islands. We know magic is not from the Great One. Her magic may bring good for a while, but the end of a person practicing magic is always sad and lonely and frightening."

"Yes" said Dendal, "This is the deception of magic."

Dodo nodded and continued, "One day we managed to tie her up and threw her magic spells books into a fire. She was helpless, tied up, but she had one magic book left that we are still looking for. We cannot find it, and with the power left in that one book, she hexed us and cursed out a spell that all of us would be under deception. Her curse was that we would always be fighting among ourselves finally to destroy each other and ourselves."

"What an awful curse!" exclaimed Sasha.

Dodo nodded and said, "When I heard her calling out the chants, I called for help from The Great One and I never came under the spell. Sadly, my nineteen friends did not call for help and they came under the spell!"

Dendal said gravely, "The Great One is for all the people, whoever calls on His name will get help at that moment, only thing, we have to remember to call Him for help."

Dodo said, "I am delighted to finally meet people who understood about the Great One. It was so lonely for me all these years and I used to tell my nineteen friends about the Great One but they did not really listen to me."

Tara said, "You were protected for a greater purpose!"

Dodo said, "The greater hope keeps me going. Well, then after burning the witch's books, her giant vulture suddenly flew down and pecked at her ropes and she jumped on his back and flew away fast. That one magic book remains in this island and until it is removed and destroyed, none in the island are completely free from her curse. I am searching for the magic book to destroy it and her power. My fear is that the witch will come back again for that magic book of hers and if she does, she will destroy us as well as many more people."

Akim said, "This is terrible, the book must be found to be destroyed or it will harm more people."

Dodo nodded and said, "Exactly, I have been trying to find that book for a long time, but I cannot find it. She also cast a spell on the pear tree, that whoever eats the magic pears will become mad. The curse of the pear tree can be broken and my nineteen friends can be free from the curse by someone who has to say certain words. This can happen even if we do not find the magic book. I am still waiting for that one person to come and break their curse."

"Maybe we can find the magic book and use it for good instead of bad?" suggested Bravo.

Dodo looked at him sternly and said with almost a rebuke. "The source of ALL magic comes from the Dark Arts. The Dark Arts is a magic that controls people to cause them harm and cast binding spells on them. Magic is also used to do "good things" like heal people etc., and this is called White Magic, but it's origin is from the Dark Arts given by the Price of Darkness to take people away from the Great One, away from the Truth and the Light. At the very end of life, even if magic brought someone great power and they performed great miracles and even healing, as the source is from the Prince of Darkness witches and wizards, it always has bad consequences."

King Asa, his men, and the others shuddered and the Star Men and Tara nodded wisely.

Akim said, "I'm beginning to under the dangers of magic, it seems good in face, but is bad in heart. Its ultimate plan is to take away people from the Truth and the Light."

Tara said, "Exactly Akim, we never use magic. We use our own abilities, gifts and talents that the Great One gives us. The Great One lights a flame within us to give us power to do great wonders through Him, but we always look to Him. We never look to the Dark Arts, Black Magic or even White Magic because in the end, these take us away from The Great One and away from the Golden Land."

"Well spoken Dodo!" said the Grinko, "You definitely know The Great One because many secrets of The Great One are revealed to you!"

Sasha exclaimed, "This is amazing, this is exactly what was shown to me when I saw the other Golden Book from the sky, the flame in our heart gives us strength to go on, and now you are saying exactly the same thing!"

Taras smiled and said, "Truth always links together to confirm it is not a lie. The lie scatters and makes people more aggressive and violent, and they hurt people. The Truth of the Great One never lets people hurt each other!"

King Asa said slowly, "I understand what you are saying Dodo. Let me tell you all something that happened in the Island of Tipukut years ago. There was a school, and one night, a group of seven girls decided to play a game by indulging in the Black Arts. They thought they were having great fun. They had invited a spirit from the second heavens to tell them their futures.

In the middle of the game, the spirit announced that "Della" one of the girls would die the next day. The girls were suddenly afraid and the game of the spirits was over. The next morning, the girls ran and told their parents about this who shared this with me. Well, we all asked the Great One to help us. That evening, Della nearly had an accident, but because the Great One helped us, nothing could touch her. The seven girls never dabbled with magic after this!"

Everyone listened in wonder to this story with racing hearts and Dodo said, "A happy ending to what could have been a disaster!"

They then walked further and saw a great lawn of soft grass, where the other dwarves were walking, and some carrying buckets of water. At the corner of the mansion, there was a huge kitchen where some of the dwarves were cooking some food with a delicious aroma.

Suddenly, they all jumped up and screamed at each other, "You stole that cutlet!" yelled the dwarf cook to another dwarf, "You took it right under my nose."

"No!" shouted the other dwarf, "You liar! I never took it. What would I do with your silly cutlet?"

"You called me a LIAR?" roared the cook in fury. "You nasty creature, you… you…scallywag!"

The dwarf yelled in fury, "You insulted me, you called me a scallywag, apologize at once!"

The cook laughed and said rudely, "Never!"

Dodo said sadly, "The thing is, they are under a fault-finding spell. If someone steps on their toe, they think the other one did it on purpose. If they cannot find something, they are certain one of them stole it. They immediately blame each other for everything.

It is a deceptive spell of perception of how negatively they perceive everything. They see the world as dismal, ugly and even when they eat the food, they find it horrible. This is a dreadful fault-finding spell, where nothing is right in their eyes, no one is okay, and they cannot see any good."

"Oh…that is so sad!" gasped Sasha, "how can we help, I mean, they are angry, but they are under a spell."

Hearing those words, Dodo jumped up with joy exclaiming, "All these years, I was waiting for a kind-hearted girl to break the spell. You are that girl who can break the spell!"

Everyone was proud that Sasha was to break the spell.

"What shall I do?" asked Sasha helplessly.

"First," replied Dodo, "You have to collect all the pears in the enchanted tree and make a little fire."

Dodo took out a roll of paper from his pocket and gave it to Sasha, "This can only be read aloud by you to break the spell, burn the pears along with this paper after reading it. We will help you collect the pears; you have to do the rest."

All of them got together, plucking the delicious juicy pears. "Be careful," warned Dodo, "these are enchanted pears, they will tempt you and you will want to eat them, but if you do, you will fall under many spells!'

They finally got all the pears in a pile, and then Akim said, "Wait!" I think we need to cut down the tree!"

No one questioned Akim, it seemed the right thing to do, and Dodo got out huge axes and some of them helped to cut down the tree.

Then Dendal said something wise, "I think we need to dig out the roots, a bad tree has bad roots and bad roots are the source of all wickedness!"

They all agreed and after cutting down the tree, proceeded to dig out the roots, and then suddenly Bravo stubbed his toe against something hard near the tree and gave out a yell.

"Oh no, I got stubbed badly!" Everyone rushed to see, thinking he had stubbed it on a root. They then noticed a bit of a box sticking out from under the soil. They took spades, dug fast, and soon took out a black box. On opening it, they found a gray book, which had ugly gray light emanating from it.

"The magic book!" called out everyone surprised.

Dodo was delighted. "Now we can burn this book along with the enchanted pears and the curse of the magic on these islands will be broken forever!"

Dodo took the magic book along with the enchanted pears and told Sasha to arrange twigs and logs, gave her two white stones, and told her to rub them together to start a fire. Soon a little flame burst forth growing into a roaring fire. Sasha took the piece of paper then solemnly read the chant:

"When nineteen dwarves are under the spell that sees all wrong

Dodo the dwarf has to remain patient and strong
The spell one day will be broken
By someone with a kind heart
And to outer darkness, the spell will forever depart"

They put the magic book and the pears in the fire; they started to crackle, burst and burn with the peach juices running through the fire. A strange green-silver fire started to glow, unlike the normal orange fire flames. It shone eerily and made a strange hissing sound like a snake.

Everyone was alarmed, but the Star Men looked at it calmly and Starrho said, "This is part of the process, be still and watch."

The green-silver fire was frighteningly beautiful, sinister and the strange hissing was sending shivers down everyone's spines.

Bravo said a little nervously, "Hope the witch does not jump out of the fire suddenly!"

Dodo shook his head and said "Impossible, she will run for miles if she sees this. This fire means her power is broken!"

As the fire glowed and grew larger and larger, everyone had to move further away. All the dwarves stopped working and watched the fire in silent amazement.

Then something queer happened. All nineteen dwarves dropped down on the grass still and lifeless as if they were dead!

Everyone were horrified and looked at Dodo who looked as horrified as they did.

Starrho made his way gingerly to the dwarves and the others followed solemnly.

Dodo started crying softly. Alas, his nineteen friends were dead! In the air of gloom, King Asa said, "We are sorry for the sad untimely demise of the dear dwarves and…"

Just then, one of the dwarf's opened one eye and said, "Eh! You are proclaiming our obituaries?"

Dodo cried out "Wodi, you are alive!'

All the dwarves started rolling over groaning in pain. They sat up holding their heads, saying their heads were feeling very heavy. Then after a while, clouds of smoke rose out of dwarves with a strange hissing sound, and lifted up and disappeared in thin wisps of white smoke. Everyone watched fascinated. Something nasty had left the dwarves.

They all jumped up shouting happily, "We are feeling lighter, as if something has left us!"

Everyone was thrilled that the dwarves were finally free, especially Dodo, grinning ear to ear. He got his friends back.

Wodi said to Dodo, "I got you, you were crying, I know you care for us!"

Dodo replied, "Yes of course, I care for all of you, but I was not crying, those were onions in my eyes!"

The cook laughed and said, "I could say onions, not you Dodo, just admit you love us so much and can't live without us!"

"Come on everybody, time for a feast," called out another dwarf happily. He along with the other dwarves had got the table ready.

Everyone was hungry and made way to a long table covered with a white cloth. On it was the most delicious food, hot and steaming, savory accompanied by sweet juicy fruits.

"Don't worry, friends;" assured the dwarves to the others, "These are not enchanted, but normal fresh fruits from our island garden."

During the meal, the team explained their mission, to go to the Island of Darkness and help the inhabitants there. The dwarves listened engrossed and said, "This is not an easy mission. You are brave folks, helping people you don't even know even as you have helped us. May your mission be successful."

"Thank you dear dwarves, we need your good wishes" said King Asa.

After eating, King Asa said, "Thank you so much wonderful friends for your kind hospitality, you must also visit our island sometime, however, our ship has sunk. Would you be kind enough to lend us a boat? We will surely return with some payment as we have lost all our supplies at sea."

"O King" replied Dodo, "We do owe you for all the help, we will certainly give you a new ship, no need to return it, I do insist, it is a gift."

After the meal, the dwarves insisted that they rest the night in the island.

"'Tis evening," said the head cook dwarf, Dwight, "If you leave in the dawn of day, it will be good and you would reach the Island of Darkness before nightfall."

Therefore, they rested in the island for the night in the huge house, which had several comfortable bedrooms. As Tara and Sasha were going to one of the guest rooms in the big house, Akim said sleepily, "Goodnight Sasha, you saved the day, you are a heroine!"

"We all did it together," replied Sasha generously, "Without each of you all, I could not do anything. We all need each other; none of us could do anything without each other." Tara and Sasha went to their comfortable beds and both hit the sack within minutes and soon were dreaming good dreams.

King Asa, the Star Men, Akim and Bravo spent some time talking in their huge guest room. Captain Soto and his crew had another huge room and went off to sleep tired after the long night and day's adventure.

In the pink of dawn the next morning, after giving a light breakfast and tea, the dwarves showed the way to a huge blue ship with magnificent white sails called Sea Bird. Everyone gasped, "Oh no, you cannot possibly do that!" said King Asa, "This ship is far too grand, we cannot take such an expensive gift!"

All the dwarves chimed in, "We do insist O King!" With all your help, the enchantment of the island is broken which brought us under the curse. Now, we are no longer calling this Enchanted Island, but Sunrise Island!"

"Great name!" said Zora, the Star Man, "Sunrise with a fresh beginning!"

As they led them to the ship, Dodo and the dwarves carried bags and bags of food and fresh water and gave each of the team a small golden-wrapped gift. "This is a personal gift, to remember us and it will come in handy," said Dodo. After the farewells, the team entered the beautiful ship.

As they said goodbye, King Asa said solemnly, "Thank you so much wonderful friends for your kind hospitality. We will return one day again!"

The dwarves were glad to know that King Asa and his team were going to make another trip to the island. They said their goodbyes and watched the crew leaving on the beautiful new ship and sail out into the pink beautiful dawn.

Chapter 12
The Island of Darkness

As they resumed sailing, the seagulls cried over them and the waters danced merrily in the sun. Later, as they opened their gifts and all of them got a tiny golden lantern, which looked very pretty, glowing with golden light. Everyone was delighted with the gifts.

Starrho remarked, "There is something unusual about this gift. It is not just a pretty lamp; there is something more to it."

Akim asked with interest, "What do you think it is Starrho?"

Starrho said, "Time will tell what these lamps really are, but these are not ordinary lamps."

King Asa said, "The dwarves are amazing, I cannot imagine how generous they are, the ship is magnificent, I was expecting a little boat, but this is very grand, I will have to go back to the island and repay them again."

The hours rolled by, the sun got hotter. The Star Men, King Asa, and the children went to their cabins.

Captain Soto and the sailors' compass pointed east to the Island of Darkness.

Suddenly, as they were sitting peacefully, a huge black rat ran across Akim's feet. Akim cried out, "Ouch, a rat!"

Captain Soto saw it and yelled out "That scallywag is back again, it looks the same one as before. It seems it followed us to the island when our ship sunk, must have got on the raft, and now is back again in the new ship…little pest, throw it out!"

The rat sneakily hid into a corner and disappeared through a wooden plank.

As the ship sailed forward, a strong breeze helped the ship to sail faster eastward.

Ro, the sailor smiled and said, "It seems all is well and there is a fair wind propelling us forward eastward in favor of us. We will definitely reach before sunset."

In fact, within a couple of hours, they saw about 4 miles ahead an ugly dense fog hanging over an island. An abysmal sense of gloom hung over the island and everyone in the ship shuddered.

Just then, unexpectedly, an albatross encircled the ship and flew like an ominous shadow. The sailors shuddered.

Ro exclaimed, "It is a curse and a boon to see an albatross near the ship!"

Starrho looked at Ro and said, "We should not live in the fear of curses because when we have the Great One with us, He breaks every curse."

Akim added, "I agree on that one, I have seen the power of the curse broken on the dwarves' island!"

"Ask the Great One for help, folks, we really need it, we are nearing the island. It does not look good ahead!" said King Asa.

Everyone quietly called on The Great One. They did not know exactly what they were supposed to do, but as the Crier said, as the time approached, The Great One would show them.

Tara said quietly, "This is an important part of the journey; something important has to be fulfilled in the Island of Darkness, thought it seems unpleasant, we have to go through it and only then we have the power over the darkness."

Dendal said, "Exactly, Tara, you always hit the nail on the head!"

Billho said, "Welcome to the darkness...to an unknown fate."

Grinko said, "Correction Grinko, we are not in the hands of fate, fate can be cruel sometimes, we are under the care of the Great One, nothing can happen to us."

Billho did not look too certain, this was his first Earth mission and he did not like the mist and gloom of the Island of Darkness and the forbidding atmosphere.

Zora saw his face and said, "Cheer up, Billho, it won't be so bad, we are the conquerors always, remember?"

Billho nodded and Akim patted Billho and said, "Billho, we will bring the light to this island!"

Akim did not know what made him say that but he felt he had said the right thing.

As they came closer to the island, they noticed huge birds flying around silently. Finally, they reached the shore, and they anchored the ship near the island and the crew got off, Starrho suddenly told, "Wear your jackets, it is cold, and carry their lantern gifts."

What a strange request thought Akim silently. The others also looked surprised but no one questioned Starrho. They each had a tiny silken bag, a gift from Dodo and they put their lanterns inside it and headed out into the dark island. As they stepped out, a cold draft immediately struck them and they shivered and held their jackets tightly around them.

"Brrrr" said Sasha, "It's really cold here!"

They did not see inhabitants. It was silently sinister with the shrill cries of the birds. They could hardly see ahead of them. The Star Men could not glow in the fog.

Then Bravo got a brain wave and said, "Lets light our lanterns!"

"What!" scoffed Sasha, "They will not work in this thick fog!"

"One can never tell," said Bravo, "I've seen unexpected things happen when I least expect it." He took out a matchbox, lit his lantern and then lit the others' lanterns too. The lanterns shone very brightly in the dark.

"Great idea Bravo," said King Asa, "I thought these were pretty gifts but never expected them to shine so brightly."

They noticed a little figure, hurrying in the mist, wearing a huge overcoat. He saw them and scowled, "Who are you people?" He looked especially strangely at the Star Men who did look different, tall, thin and silvery with a very faint silver shine around them. He glared at Tara, for some reason, he took a dislike to Tara.

"Good evening, we are visitors in your island," answered King Asa politely.

"We do not welcome visitors!" snapped the little man, shrouded in his dark coat with his face barely seen.

"Leave them alone!" shouted another voice. They saw an old shadowy man, leaning on a stick.

The old man said, "Hello strangers, what do you want?"

Then to their surprise, they heard hundreds of voices saying, "Who are you, who are you, who are you."

The team turned around, stunned to see hundreds of tiny shadowy people, shrouded in huge overcoats. Most of them looked mean and bad-tempered, a few looked tired, and some others looked timid. None of them looked happy, but they did not seem overly dangerous. They remembered the Crier's words, "You cannot help those who do not want to be helped."

A shadowy woman came near them and hissed, "You all better be gone before our prince finds you. He will surely eat you for his dinner!"

"Come on," called out the other little people, "Our prince is not that bad, in fact, he is good, he is wonderful, and he is the best. He would never harm these invaders."

The shadowy woman said to the others in a whining tone, "Tell these horrid people to go away. Those terrible lanterns they are carrying are hurting my eyes. I tell you, once the prince comes, he will be furious with such wretches on our precious island. They are trespassing!"

The shadowy man in the massive huge overcoat walked up to them hobbling with his stick and said, "I think you are welcome, you seem kind of nice people, come on to my little hut!"

The shadowy woman hissed at him "You fool, nincompoop! Do you realize you are welcoming intruders on our island? We never welcome strangers, you know that!"

The man answered her "Our prince is a good one; he will welcome them with open arms!"

King Asa and team were a little confused wondering who they were speaking about, when they suddenly saw a huge black figure walking up to them out of nowhere. His black cloak glistened and he looked very grand. When the people saw him, they all bowed down. He was very handsome.

They all started to bow down except the Star Men, who were not prone to the same temptations and gullibility as humans.

Akim suddenly caught a strange glimmer in the prince's black eyes, which did not seem very right. Akim snapped out of the hypnotism spell that they all seemed to be under. He remembered something he had learned earlier from the Star Men. They often said that the deceptive one sometimes comes as a being of light and goodness.

Akim called out loudly, "The deceptive one comes as a being of light, call on the Great One, everyone!"

As Akim said that, he repeated it again, and the fog seemed to clear from the teams' minds and the lanterns started to radiate very brightly.

King Asa said, "You are right Akim, we were about to be deceived, come on everyone, snap out of this trance."

Tara said, "My goodness, I nearly fell into a trap, imagine me, and I have never been deceived before, this has to be the Prince of Darkness, how foolish of me that I did not realize it before."

The sailors and crew agreed and Bravo said, "We are saved by the bell, in the right fraction of time or we would have been swallowed up!"

Sasha cried out, "O Great One, help us, we need you!"

The Star Men in unison called unto the Great One.

As they started calling, talking and even singing out aloud, glitter of lights started to fall down. As the Prince saw this, he started to yell out, "Who are you people and what are you doing on my island?"

The shadowy woman said triumphantly to the others, "See, I told you the Prince does not like strangers in our island, but you would not listen, now you pay for bitter price for your disobedience in welcoming them, we should have thrown them out the moment we saw them!"

As she was speaking, the darkness started evaporating around in the island. The shadowy woman gave a cry of terror and the Prince let out a strange-sounding wail.

In the meantime, many minds started to clear. The small shadowy people seemed less like shadows. They stopped bowing to the Prince and started looking around themselves as if awakening from a bad dream. Many of them started throwing off their overcoats as if they were throwing off a bad omen.

Seeing this, the Prince roared in anger and yelled out to the little islanders.

"These intruders are bad, do not listen to them my precious followers, they are trying to tell you lies. They will never let you become the great people you are meant to be, don't listen to their lies!"

The shadowy woman whined to the prince, "O wonderful mighty Prince, they are not listening to me. I told them to throw out these people, but they were talking to these terrible intruders and inviting them to their homes!"

The Prince said, "You did right, Shawdie, as you always do. I always said you are the most sensible of all, you will have an important place in my kingdom."

Shawdie, the woman looked pleased. She suddenly had visions of becoming the leader of lands and ruling all the other silly shadowy islanders.

The Prince called out "Hobodobosolalala" which was his enchantment spell, but he found the people's eyes had brightened and the fogginess that was hanging over their heads had disappeared.

Again, Akim called out words he remembered from what Dendal had shared with him once, "The deceptive one has blinded the minds of those who do not believe!"

Akim shouted loudly, "BE FREE!" A great light appeared and hung over the island. It was pure glistening white light and shone through the island. Most of the island people now wanted the pure light. They saw the difference between the two and found the glistening white light beautiful but not dazzling. They called out for the light as the fogginess was leaving their minds.

When the Prince saw and heard this, he started screaming at them again, his face contorted, purple and ugly, "You buffoons, nincompoops and rascals!"

The islanders were surprised because they had never heard the prince speaking with them so rudely nor had they seen such a hysterical wild version of him. Speechlessly they watched him.

The old man said softly to the others, "I always knew something was wrong, but I could never place it, but now I know, the Prince is really vile and he has kept us in blindness."

Many of the people around the old man called Manjo agreed and said, "Manjo, you are so wise, we are seeing a different prince, and it is so frightening!"

The Prince heard them speaking and was enraged. He kept turning around in circles. He could not bear the light around him. He was the Prince of Darkness. The Great One's light made him feel terrible and horrible and he wanted to get away fast.

Then he gave everyone a frightful shock! He transformed himself into a hideous looking monster, gave a howl of rage and raised his claw-like hands as if he wanted to cast a magic evil spell on everyone. To his horror, he found his magic did not work as more light was infiltrating the Island of Darkness. He covered his red glaring eyes with his scaly hands and with a scream of fury, he rose and flew out of the island with big bat-like wings.

He kept shrieking shrilly "I'll come back and kill you all, wait and see, you traitors and Manjo, you will get it the worst for deceiving the others!"

No one knew how he suddenly developed into a monster with wings! All the people in the Island of Darkness were still in a daze to see the hideous change in the Prince of Darkness who always looked so charming and handsome.

Manjo, the old man with the stick said, "I cannot imagine how we did not realize what an evil one the Prince is, and I am not afraid of his threats. He is calling evil good and good evil, that is what I realized of the Prince today!"

Most of the others agreed, realizing that they were actually worshipping someone so evil who transformed himself into beauty but was a hideous creature in reality.

Dendal, the Star Man said to the islanders, "Don't worry, he is never going to return to the island. He cannot bear the Light in the island. Keep the Light always inside the island and nothing will happen to you."

There were a group of small islanders who could not bear the light either and felt like running away too. Some of them were groaning loudly, "Turn off this light, it is hurting us, we can't bear it!"

Shawdie said, "Let's all get away from this horrible light and go somewhere else, get your belongings and boats ready, I am sure the Prince will come and help us wherever we go!"

Manjo called out, "Shawdie, you are deceived, the Prince is lying to you, in the end, after using you, he will destroy you, wake up Shawdie before he finishes you off!"

Transformed Island

Then, a Voice was heard out of the darkness, powerful, deep, strong and kind saying, "You are no longer the Island of Darkness but the Island of Light," and the Voice continued, "Well done, my children!"

The team knew who was speaking to them, the Great One! Everyone thought of beautiful things when they heard His Voice. The islanders were astonished. They somehow knew this was king far greater than their prince was.

However, as some others, Shawdie, the woman could not bear the light and the Voice. She shrieked like a banshee when she heard the Voice, screaming, "That horrible terrible Voice. Shut it up!"

She then closed her ears and wobbled off far away. Some other mean-looking people in huge overcoats agreed with her and yelled out, "Leave us in peace. You came to our island to disturb us. We were happy and now you brought that horrible voice and that bright ugly light."

These were people of the Darkness. About a hundred of them quickly ran out with bags of belongings and jumped into little boats to escape. They all went together. They formulated a plan to live together in another island. They, however, were worried whether that island would be too bright for them to live in.

Shawdie screamed at the other islanders as she hobbled to a boat, "You horrible folks, you turned away from our dear prince, unfaithful wretches, you wait and see, I will come back with greater powers and get you, my prince has promised me great power and I will destroy you all with that power!"

Manjo shouted back, "Did you see what a hideous creature our handsome prince really is, Shawdie? How can you still follow him?"

Shawdie replied, "It proves what power he has, he has power to turn into anything. You wait and see, he will come back and destroy you all, I will come with him and I will have the last laugh!"

The little folks cried out, "Shawdie, you are insanely following an evil ruler, you cannot see anything wrong in him even if he was the most evil one on Earth!"

Shawdie and the others glared at everyone and then hurriedly jumped into their boats.

The other island people did seem to mind them going because they were so happy. All rejoiced and declared the Voice as the Great One to rule them.

The team solemnly handed out a book that had truth in it. They needed to read it every morning. They gratefully chose the one among them who had the kindest heart and the strongest voice to read the instructions and comforting words from the book.

Starrho said, "I vote we leave now as our mission is over and we have to start immediately as the weather is clearing. Is that okay with everyone?"

"No, no, please join us for a piping hot traditional island dinner." The islanders said, "We want to celebrate, and spend some time with you. We have nice bamboo huts that you can sleep in tonight."

"Alright," said King Asa, "We will stay the night and we will head out in the sea the next morning when the weather was pleasant."

The islander gave them a delicious dinner of rice, tender bamboo shoots, tender green leaf vegetables, fried fish and a delicious tomato curry and sweet juicy fruits to follow.

After dinner, the Star Men and Tara taught the islanders how they were to live their new lives. The stars above seem to twinkle very merrily at their conversation.

Early the next morning, the team left, promising to return some day. The Star Men, King Asa, Akim, Tara, Sasha and Bravo and others headed back in sea and on looking back, they saw a shining light hanging over the island.

Tara exclaimed, "This is wonderful, we overcame the darkness and brought light into the island?"

Dendal said solemnly, "The light shines in the darkness and the darkness cannot overcome it, but the light overcomes the darkness!'

Sasha said happily, "I have many exciting adventures to share with my parents when we get back!"

Akim agreed and said, "This will be the most wonderful time that Dora Valley will have, when we all get back, King Asa, Tara, Bravo, and Sasha and everyone else, and of course our dear Star Men, you must come too at least for one big banquet before you get home. It will be a time of great sharing."

Starrho nodded and said, "That time together sound wonderful. This is when we can teach the others about the Golden Book also, good idea Akim!"

King Asa said smiling "The Island of Darkness is transformed to an island of light, what a victory and of course, we will all gather in Dora Valley, this is where it all started!"

Chapter 13
The City of Skilk and the Woman

Something Happens to Akim

The ship started to sail towards the direction of the City of Skilk. They sailed the whole day and by evening, the moon arose and hundreds of stars scattered in the sky.

Starrho looked at the Star Men and Akim and said softly. "The time is close; we are nearing the City of Skilk. I can feel it! Once we reach, we will scout the land and find out the whereabouts of the green snake. The time has come to fly in the sky again."

All agreed heartily. They had obeyed to Great One's command to help those who needed help along the way, but the mission was nearing and time was at hand.

King Asa said, "Bye all, we will be heading back to the Island of Tipukut. See you all someday."

Akim said, "When this mission is over, you must come to Dora Valley, King Asa."

King Asa said, "We will meet together in Dora Valley, as I promised."

After all their goodbyes, they watched the Star Men, Akim, Tara and Sasha rise up and fly in the sky. King Asa, Bravo, Captain Soto and his team of sailors looked a little sad to see their company of friends leaving. They were very silent as they were steering the Sea Bird back to the Island of Tipukut.

In the meantime, the Star Men looked towards the stars and flew up, holding Akim, Tara and Sasha under the force of a warm wind that protected them from falling. They actually went to sleep as they were flying, while the Star Men kept flying in the direction of the harbors of the City of Skilk.

Finally, at dawn, they spotted a city port with hundreds of little boats, ships and people. Tara, Sasha and Akim got up with a start. They had never seen so many people together at one time.

Tara said in wonder, "This was how the City of Skilk was described to me, I never thought I would be here one day, now please stick together and don't take any help from strangers, we can't trust anyone here."

Sasha said, "I have never seen so many people, seems like millions of people, armies of people all over, it's kind of scary."

Akim was strangely silent and the Star Men glanced at him.

They flew down swiftly and landed on the port with a thud. Akim kept rubbing his eyes, he felt extremely sleepy as he had not slept properly a few nights.

Zora said, "Welcome folks to the City of Skilk! Now this is the actual spot of action and adventure."

Billho said looking around, "Seems this is the most action place on Earth, looks kind of overcrowded."

Grinko said, "The people are hurrying all around, and no one even seems to notice us. It's nice not to be stared at for a change!"

The City of Skilk never slept! Thousands of people were walking around in that early morning hour, it seemed hundreds of fishermen were setting out in little boats to catch fish, food stalls were steaming with hot tea and early morning breakfast, women venders were setting up their stalls for jewelry bangles, clips, jasmine-scented flowers, roses, and many other commodities. Though trade, commerce, business was flourishing, they noticed many hungry looking ragged children running around, old women begging and lots of dirt lying around. Akim had never seen beggars in Dora Valley.

Sasha said, "What a sad city, I thought the City of Skilk would be a grand great city, not this human sea of bustle!"

"Indeed, a sad city" said Piran, then he glanced at Akim and said, "Are you okay, Akim? You are so silent!"

Akim mumbled something incomprehensible. His bones were aching and he felt cramped. He also suddenly felt very homesick. He longed for the comfort of his home with Uncle Jon and Aunt Nelly and longed for a hot shower, to sleep in his own bed and eat his home food. Akim suddenly felt queer and feverish.

He heard Starrho say, "We need to find an inn in order to find out more information about the Green Snake as in inns, one meets people who talk a lot."

As they walked into the city, Zora exclaimed, "There is an inn, it looked crowded, so there will be lots of people that we can find out things from.

Starrho said, "This is perfect, here we would meet plenty of people, nice and crowded, and we can have some tea to start with!"

Akim's heart sank as they entered the inn. The sound of clattering and chatting hurt Akim's ears as people noisily ate breakfast and drank mugs of steaming hot tea.

Akim looked at Starrho and said, "I don't want to stay in this inn, it is so noisy and crowded. I want something quiet, I need to sleep, and I feel sort of ill."

Starrho said soothingly, "We'll get you to the room immediately so you can rest, Akim."

Akim replied his voice quivering slightly, "I don't want to stay here. I am going to look for another inn."

Tara, Sasha and the Star Men stared at Akim, surprised. He was not the same gentle Akim they knew.

Wise Dendal said gently, "Akim must be feeling really ill, he needs immediate rest."

Akim shook his head and said, "I'm going to look for another inn and I will call you there too, I need something more peaceful, I hate this noise."

Starrho said surprised, "Akim, don't go, let's stay together or you will get lost."

Tara said, "Akim, remember, we have to stick together, this is crucial in this part of the journey. Come on Akim, we are all here now finally, isn't it amazing we made it this far crossing all our troubles?"

Akim did not answer. He stood up thinking indignantly *This, Starrho always decides everything for everyone, but the Great One chose **me** to recover the Golden Book, I am important too. It's time they also listened to me. I'm the main one here!"*

These churning thoughts Akim were alien to him as he was generally very humble, patient, and gentle. Yet, today, he was a different Akim. He suddenly marched out of the inn, and the others tried to call him but he did not turn around and the others stared after him in dismay. They did not see where he went because he quickly disappeared into the crowd.

"Oh dear!" cried Grinko distressed. "Where can he be, he will get lost!"

Everyone tried to look for Akim, but they could not find him because he vanished into the sea of crowd.

"Dear, dear," said Sasha, "I have never seen Akim like this, he is so calm and gentle and cheerful all the time."

Tara said, "It is the stress and tiredness of the journey, at the end of it all, sometimes folks break down, but we got to find him fast."

"Let's wait here in the inn," suggested Piran, "He will definitely come back and if we move from here, we will all lose each other."

They waited, and waited, until they felt something was definitely wrong. They then decided to go and search for him.

Akim and the Lady

As Akim marched out, he was angry. He was angry with Starrho and Dendal for making all the decisions when he knew the Great One had chosen him for the great task. He was also tired, hungry and he actually felt a little strange in the City of Skilk. There were stalls, shops, people, noise and confusion everywhere.

As he kept walking, he came to a little clearing with a little bench near the sea, which had a patch of grass around. A huge tree hung over the bench and he sat down tiredly looking out at the sea waves. He closed his eyes saying indignantly to himself, "What a bossy person Starrho is, and Dendal too…always deciding everything, they never consult me ever though the Great One has chosen me for the mission…I will show them… I will…" With those words, he fell asleep dreaming unpleasant dreams and he tossed and turned on the bench when suddenly, something touched him and he awoke with a start. He looked around him and got a whiff of a lovely scent, he looked up to see a beautiful woman smiling down at him sweetly. Next to her was a huge gleaming black carriage driven by two magnificent silver horses. She touched him again lightly with a long sparkling silver stick that she held in her hand.

"Hello little boy," she said in a soft silvery voice that sounded like a tinkling stream, "You look tired, lost and also new in the city. I do hope you are not lost, I don't like to see children lost; I have not seen you in these parts of the city."

"Yes Ma'am, I am new in the city," said Akim, in awe that she was speaking with him. She looked noble, like a queen with a silken green gown, shiny brown hair with the clearest skin Akim had ever seen.

"Come on child, you can come to my house to rest. I always help guests in the City of Skilk, I will give you something to eat and drink as well."

Akim was grateful and he got into her gleaming black carriage, which had silken green curtains and soft silken green cushions. He was very comfortable and happy and he had forgotten all about the Star Men.

The grand lady asked him, "Where do you come from little boy?"

Akim answered, "I come from a valley very far from here, called Dora Valley."

The lady exclaimed, "Amazing, you came from so far away, did you come by ship?"

Akim replied, "Partly by ship and we flew partly."

The lady gave a little squeal of delight and exclaimed, "This is amazing, fancy flying, you must be magic!"

Akim replied, "Not really, we don't use magic."

The lady enquired, "And who might be "we" little boy."

Akim replied vaguely, "Well, my friends."

Akim suddenly felt guilty. He had forgotten all about the Star Men, Tara and Sasha.

Finally, they arrived at a beautiful grand white mansion with an enormous garden.

Akim thought, "This is the grand life of royalty. This is why the Great One chose me. He wanted me to get to know royalty and to become royalty. This is wonderful; I could become great like this one day and rule a kingdom, perhaps one day I will rule the City of Skilk!"

Akim told the grand lady a little timidly, "Please can I have a hot shower?"

The lady said graciously, "Of course, my dear child, you must."

After a steaming hot shower, Akim felt very relaxed and comfortable. The lady then took Akim to a huge room with beautiful green curtains, soft sinking sofas. She made him sit on a grand chair and gave him a warm sweet drink and food that he had never tasted before, but was delicious.

She said, "I know you must be hungry and tired. This food and will soothe your tired nerves, and you can sleep a while and later I will take you to meet some very important people in the city. I see you have royalty written in your face, and you must meet these people."

Akim replied respectfully and in awe "Thank you your majesty!"

She showed him to a huge room with a soft comfortable bed, within minutes Akim was fast asleep.

It was hours later that Akim awakened to a chilly icy blast of cold air. He tried to sit up but found to his horror that he was tied!

"I can't believe this, I am tied up!" he cried out in dismay and fear. "Oh who would do such a thing to me, where is that lady, I need to call her to help me."

He called out weakly, "O lady, please help me!"

There was silence and Akim thought *Oh, why didn't I listen to Starrho and the others? Oh, what happened to me?*

Suddenly he started in shock. He saw the beautiful lady standing in the corner of the room and Akim exclaimed in relief, "Oh, so glad to see you again, I don't know who tied me up, please untie me!"

The lady did not say a word but she stood watching him and she suddenly did not look quite so beautiful!

Akim suddenly wondered in horror, *Did she tie me up? But why!!*

Akim asked her in a quivering voice "Did you tie me?"

The lady replied coldly, "Yes."

Akim asked her in bewilderment, "Why did you tie me?"

She said, "Do you remember the Enchanted Island? You destroyed my power. This is my moment of revenge."

Akim asked her in astonishment, "You are the witch?"

The woman laughed and said, "Yes indeed, and after I flew off on my vulture, I went to the Prince of Darkness and he invested greater powers in me. I saw the prophecy on you that you will destroy the darkness. I was waiting for you all, I knew about your ship journey ever since you all went to the Enchanted Island and I had my spies watching you. The Seekers were always watching you though they were instructed not to harm, but to inform me of your travels. When all of you arrived in the City of Skilk, I knew immediately you had arrived. I will not let you destroy any more of my kingdom. I am going to hand you and get the others too and hand you all over to the Prince of Darkness and he will finish you."

Akim asked, "Why would he want us?"
The witch replied, "He said he wanted to keep all of you as his slave for the distress you and your silly team caused him in the Island of Darkness and my revenge is the distress you caused me in the Enchanted Island by destroying my magic book. I will hunt the others out too and bring them to the Prince of Darkness!" She laughed cruelly and walked out of the room.

Akim called after her bravely, "Why do you follow the Prince of Darkness when you know he is evil. He is only using you and in the end, he will take you to a horrible gray place, you are only being fooled by him!"

The witch laughed evilly and said, "You people say that because you are all weak. The Prince of

Darkness gives me great power, greater than any of you
can ever have."

She walked out and slammed the door shut
locking it firmly after her. Akim suddenly missed the
Star Men, Tara and Sasha very badly. He was ashamed of
his outburst and longed for them. He thought, *They were
so kind, wise, gentle and humorous at all times.* He gave
a sigh. He remembered how the Prince of Darkness had
turned into a monster, and he was sure the witch too in
reality was a hideous monster in the garb of beauty.

*Beauty is in the inside, not the outside t*hought
Akim. *Someone can be so beautiful outside but really
ugly and hideous inside and one day, that ugly inside will
show up and shock us all*!

Akim tried to untie his hands but could not. He
was a miserable prisoner in a huge beautiful cold room.
Akim shuddered at the truth of this and tried to think of
something to cheer himself up and a song popped up in
his mind. He remembered Aunt Nelly who always told
him to sing a happy song when he was afraid and he
started to sing softly:

> *"Peace! be strong!*
> *Nothing will go wrong*
> *The right door will open*
> *With the right key*
> *Then, all the evil will flee!"*

He kept singing the words, and the more he sang,
a comfort filled him and the clutching fear started to leave
him. He suddenly heard a sound at the corner of the room
and started, looking hard at the corner.

He saw a hearth, sooty and black and then emerging from the hearth were two figures sooty and black, the whites of their eyes gleaming fiercely in their sooty faces! Akim's heart pounded wildly.

"Monsters have come down from the chimney, the Prince of Darkness's monsters, oh no, I am doomed and dead!" he watched in terror as the monsters walked towards him. As they nearly touched Akim, he gave a yell, and then one monster spoke and said, "Hello Akim!" Akim started hard at the monsters and then cried out in delight "Grinko and Zora dear friends, you came!"

"Shhhh!" said Grinko and they both quickly untied Akim, and quietly led him towards the hearth. Just as they stepped inside the hearth concealed by the chimney, the door opened and the beautiful lady aka witch walked in.

When she saw that Akim was gone, she gave a scream of rage! Her face looked contorted and ugly at that moment and Akim watching her from the chimney wondered how he ever thought she was beautiful.

She is really very ugly inside and that is what I am outside seeing now, he thought. *How foolish I was.* They heard her screaming, "Where is that boy! Where is he?"

Her helpers came running into the room and they looked around the room. The witch searched the room frantically, looked frenzied and mad with her hair flying all over. As she came near the fireplace, Akim's heart was in his mouth. He was afraid that she would drag them out, but she did not seem to notice Akim, Grinko and Zora inside the huge fireplace. It was as if she looked towards the chimney, but they were invisible to her!

She kept ranting, raving and stomping around in the room and Akim sat trembling in the chimney, holding on to Grinko and Zora's hands tightly. He wondered what made him leave the others in such anger.

After a while to their great relief, the witch and her servants left the room.

In the meantime, Grinko and Zora held Akim's hand and they gently flew through the chimney, which was quite wide actually. They flew back to the inn where the others were waiting. Fortunately, it was a starry night so Grinko and Zora were able to fly easily, carrying Akim along with their wind. Grinko and Zora took Akim upstairs in the inn to the room they had hired and the Star Men, Tara and Sasha were waiting anxiously for them.

When they saw them, they whooped in delight. Akim felt embarrassed to look at them.

The Star Men and Tara went up to Akim with joy and hugged him! Akim was astounded. This was the first hug he ever received from them and was surprised that they cared so much for him. He felt buoyant and merry and said, "I never realized you cared for me so much and I am so sorry, I really made a mess of things!"

Tara said good-naturedly, "It's alright, and off course we care for you, now come on and let's have dinner down at the inn!"

Sasha said, "I'm starving!"

Later, as they sat in the inn and ate dinner and Akim narrated the events, and told them about the witch.

Dendal whistled in surprise and said "Whew! The woman you met was actually the same witch of the Enchanted Island; that is so very strange, imagine, she is actually following us."

Akim replied, "She said the Seekers are following us, but they have instructions not to harm us because she wants to hand us over to the Prince of Darkness, who has a score to settle with us for throwing him out of the Island of Darkness."

Akim said ruefully, "I am sorry, I messed up real bad."

Starrho gently said to Akim, "Akim, sometimes after a great mission is given, as time went on, people can get tired because they stop looking to the Great One for help. Humans feel that they have all the powers within them to accomplish everything, but in humans, there is always weakness, even in the strongest ones. No single human is infallible and if they feel so, circumstances humble them. The enemy from outside did not attack you, but an enemy within and then after that, the enemy from outside took advantage of that."

Akim asked in surprise, "How within?"

Starrho replied, "You had the power to resist the witch's offers. The only way to remain strong is to talk to the Great One at that time, and to sing a song or think of something good. These are your weapons on Earth, which will help you to win any battle!"

Akim nodded and said sadly, "I really missed the mark!"

"It's okay," said Dendal, "We can all miss the mark sometimes. The important thing is to get up again and keep walking, keep going on, try again and do not remain down and never give up!"

Akim nodded gravely realizing it was an important lesson to learn. He also realized that he should never deviate from the pathway of his task. Sometimes distractions were really sent as a trap.

"Helping others along the way is different from deviating from the task," Akim suddenly announced to the others who smiled at him.

Billho said grinning, "You are beginning to get it Akim, those little sparks of wisdom!"

Chapter 14
The Invitation

That night, all of them slept peacefully in the enormous inn room. Tara and Sasha slept near the enormous windows and could see the ships in the harbor and they could even hear the sound of the waves.

Akim and the Star Men spent some time talking for a long time. Starrho said, "Now that we know both the witch and the Prince of Darkness are on the prowl for us, we need to really look out for them."

They agreed and after a while, all of them were fast asleep.

Early, the next morning, all awakened to the sound of the clamorous city din. They washed and felt refreshed and after eating breakfast, they made plans for the day.

Zora said, "Once we find out where the Green Snake is, we will find the Golden Book. A good way is by talking to the people in the city who know all that is happening. I think that the old men selling tea and coffee in open carts will know more about the city than anyone else will. They are in sync with all that is happening in the city."

Akim did not seem so sure, wondering how old vendors would know much. As they walked towards a tea vendor buying tea from him, Dendal casually struck up a conversation with the vendor, "What a beautiful city this is, we are new here, have you lived here long?"

The tea vendor nodded impatiently and almost snapped saying "Yes, yes!" It was clear he did not want to talk much and was a little irritated, so the Star Men and Akim politely left after drinking their tea.

As they wandered about the city, they seemed to have no leads, people were busy, rushing and did not want to talk to anyone, least of all strangers. Akim wistfully thought of Dora Valley and how friendly and kind everyone was, how they welcomed strangers even inviting them home.

"Cities are horrible places," he said, "People are rushed, unkind, cold and mechanical, always meeting deadlines in a business fashion. It seems human beings are second place and a nuisance if they come in anyone's way."

Tara said, "I agree with you Akim, we have more love and hospitality in small towns, people as so busy rushing around they have no time for anyone in cities."

Later in the afternoon, they were hungry and as they were walking down a street, they noticed a cheery fire crackling merrily in the distance with a black pot over it, bubbling with something. As they came closer, they got a delicious aroma wafting out of the pot.

A little old man was sitting near the pot stirring it vigorously and singing a little song happily. He looked up and smiled at them widely. The Star Men and Akim were a little startled. This was the first warm smile they received since they came to the City of Skilk. It warmed their hearts.

"Hello!" called out Billho cheerily, "How are you and may we ask your name?"

"Hello," replied the old man "I am fine thank you, my name is Dimho. Are you visitors in the City of Skilk? I know nearly every face, and I can see you have come from afar."

Starrho realized that he was a very insightful old man and perhaps the key person who could help them to find the Green Snake. He decided to let Dimho into the loop.

"Yes, we are new here; in fact, we have come on a mission!"

The others realized that the old man was a kindred soul and they did not mind Starrho sharing that information with him.

Starrho continued on smoothly, "We are looking for the Green Snake!"

Dimho was startled and looked shocked and quickly looked around. "Shhhh," he whispered fiercely, "Do not ever take that name here so loudly. Please whisper, it is dangerous to speak out that name, there are spies all around!"

Dimho cleared his throat again and said loudly, "Do join me for a meal; I have cooked some delicious stew along with fresh hot rice."

He beckoned to them to join him nearby, where they saw a little wooden house. Dimho said that cooked his food outside, as he did not have a kitchen in his tiny room, which is why he cooked his main meals outside on the wood fire.

The Star Men joined Dimho for a midday meal in his tiny one room, which had an attached bathroom. The Star Men, Akim, Tara, and Sasha kept talking to Dimho, sharing about the adventures they had and the mission they had to accomplish.

Dimho listened very carefully and said, "I know where the Green Snake is, but getting to the Green Snake is a perilous process. In fact, because of the Green Snake, the City of Skilk is in bondage."

"What do you mean by bondage?" asked Akim curiously.

"Bondage means something that ties up people's minds," replied Dimho, "This is an area where the people are in a trance, they are cold, indifferent, and always busy and rushed."

Tara said thoughtfully, "I can see that!"

Dimho continued, "The Green Snake has put that curse on them so they cannot see the Light and the Truth. They hate and reject it and call it a Lie. Only few people who embrace the Light can be broken free out of that bondage."

It sounded very grand and powerful when Dimho said it and everyone felt a kind of electricity current go through them when Dimho said it.

Starrho said, "It will be wonderful if the bondage can be broken, which is why we have to find the Green Snake. Can you tell us exactly where the Green Snake is?"

Dimho replied cautiously and very softly as if almost afraid to give this information, "He lives in a cave, but that cave is outside the city, surrounded by a thick forest. Ghouls and ghosts haunt the forest they say; no one can walk through it. There are many stories of the wild animals and evil spirits that roam around and no one can come out alive, maybe only one or two people lived to tell their horror story!"

"We are not afraid," said Zora calmly, "We, the Star Men, Tara, Akim, and Sasha have faced dangers, and overcome, and we will overcome again!" Zora, always adventurous and never afraid always decided that the outcome of everything would be victorious.

Dimho nodded, "I know, the great ones who are on a mission are never afraid. I will show you the way to the forest tonight. We cannot go during the day, but how you will get into the forest is your battle. Just be careful of Prince Skotadi, he rules this city and is a follower of the Prince of Darkness."

After the meal, the Star Men, Tara, Akim and Sasha decided to go for a little walk just to have a look at the city and as they were walking along the sidewalk, a well-dressed man with a black moustache, shaggy eyebrows and dark deep-set eyes came up to them smiling. He said, "Good afternoon, my master wishes to call you to meet him, he noticed you were new around here and wanted me to ask you to join him for a cup of tea, and just spend some time, can you please come?"

"Who is your master?" asked Dendal.

"He is a wealthy man in the city. He always is very hospitable to strangers, and of course, well you do stand out you know, with the silver sheen around you!"

The Star Men suddenly realized that their silver sheen always made people aware that they were different and people would always notice them wherever they went. Starrho looked at the others wondering whether to accept the man's invitation.

Akim shook his head, he remembered the Queen saying the same thing to him.

Zora answered instead saying softly to Starrho, "I think we should talk to a few other people before proceeding tonight, it would be good to accept, we can find out some more information!"

Starrho looked at the others and said softly, "You think we should go?"

Akim said softly, "No, we shouldn't go with him. This is how the witch called me."

Tara said, "Yes, I agree with Akim, we should not go."

However, Roko, Zora, and Billho were quite insistent that they should go with the man and Roko whispered, "We can find out more information about many things in the city, a rich man will have access to the keys to the city!"

Finally Starrho said, "Well, no harm in just checking it out and we will be back in a jiffy."

Starrho turned to the man and said, "Alright, we will come with you to meet your hospitable master."

"Thank you" said the man. He took them all in a huge blue carriage, and they all sat down comfortably while huge horses drove them driving them to a magnificent brass gate. As they drove in, they saw beautiful garden ground, full of flowers, trees and tiny colored birds flying all around an elaborate white marble palace. The master was indeed very wealthy.

As huge doors swung open, they saw uniformed guards everywhere. The Star Men, Tara, Akim and Sasha started to feel a little uncomfortable. The man led them to a big beautiful room. Seated on an enormous black silken chair was a man. He was grand, regal, wore a silken purple robe, and had jewels all over, on his fingers, neck, and flashing on his clothes.

He got up and stared at them. His eyes were coal black, penetrating and cold. Everyone shivered standing at the doorway and Akim thought, *Oh no, we made a big mistake!*

Dendal looked at everyone and whispered, "We messed up big time, and we should have not taken this invitation, sorry Akim, sorry Tara!"

Starrho whispered back, "Something definitely is not right about this mansion or the rich man."

The man on the sofa said, "What are you whispering in the corner, come on in the room, sit on the sofa all of you," he drawled. His voice was deep and powerful, yet had a chilling timber to it.
The Star Men, Tara, Akim and Sasha kept standing.
"Sit down," ordered the rich man rudely.

Just at that moment, a man stepped in the room. He was no ordinary man. He has long silver hair and a silver beard. He had a certain hue of light around him and at that moment, everyone realized he was a magician.

He did look a little familiar and Starrho gave a cry and said, "You are the same magician who attacked Bojo's cottage that night!"

The others realized the he was the same magician to their horror.

Akim said, "Now I remember your face!"

The magician sneered at them and said, "Indeed I am, and now I got you, huh, you thought you were so clever, we were watching you the whole time, our Seekers knew exactly where you were with their tentacles, they can feel where people are travelling!"

Then the realization dawned on everyone. The rich man was the prince of the city, Prince Skotadi, the follower of the Prince of Darkness as Dimho had told them! The magician was his right-hand man.

The magician looked at them and laughed and said, "Now, you all are our prisoners and gone are your powers, you are living on our mercy now!"

A sudden darkness seemed to rush into the room and suffocate everyone. The prince ordered the guards to throw them into another room.

As the strong guards caught everyone, tied them up and pushed them to another room, Prince Skotadi jeered them saying "Your mission has failed. Nothing will come out of it. Do not think you can overcome me. You are nothing; you all look ridiculous to me. I will hand you over to the Prince of Darkness tomorrow morning. Sleep your last normal night well. The Prince of Darkness will make your lives a living nightmare!"

He laughed evilly and watched them being pushed along to the other room, which was a cold bare room with a big bare window with no curtain. He locked the door. As they sat down on the cold floor, they looked at each other in trepidation.

"Do not worry," said Starrho bravely "The Great One is with us, nothing will happen, let us all talk to Him from our hearts. We made a big mistake in not talking to Him and asking His instructions before coming here, and I am sorry about that, I should have really thought about that, but let us not give up hope. Talk to Him now, it is never too late."

As they sat silently asking the Great One for help, the answer came to them startlingly crystal clear. They were to wait until evening until the stars shone in the sky. They had to find a way to open the window.

"Anyone got a pocket knife?" asked Billho.

Akim felt his pocket. He always carried a pocket knife as he enjoyed carving out figurines in wood of little ships and animals in Dora Valley. He found that a pocket knife was useful for many things needed such as cutting things, opening tins, but never had he imagined that he would need it to untie ropes from being a prisoner!

Akim gave the knife to Billho, who deftly untied himself, and then the others and they untied Akim, and then Billho leapt up towards the window, which was quite high and opened it. A cool draft came into the room.

"Shut the window, but of course do not bolt it," said Starrho, "We have to wait until evening.

The hours seem to move painfully slowly as they waited and waited and waited. By evening, the stars started to shine in the sky. Soon as a blanket of night covered the City of Skilk, the stars started to glisten more brightly.

Starrho beckoned all of them to hold hands. Just as they were about to so, the door swung open and the Grodo, the magician walked in to their shock. He looked grand and regal with his eyes gleaming and a golden hue to his skin. Powerful magicians always had a clarity glow that hung around them, but that glow was not warm but cold.

The Star Men and Akim were afraid that he being a magician would know that they were trying to escape, but the magician, Grodo did not indicate that he was aware they were trying to escape.

He looked at them coldly and said, "Tonight is your last night, tomorrow morning you will be in the hands of the Prince of Darkness, you will be his slaves and in the end, he will end you all or lock you in a dungeon forever. Did you think we were fools that we would allow you to come all the way to our city to destroy us?"

Starrho shook his head and said quietly, "Ours is not a mission of destruction, we do not believe in violence."

Grodo laughed and said, "You are definitely planning to overthrow Prince Skotadi, which is your mission, it cannot be done without violence. Violence, power, force, and money are the only way to get anything done on Earth today."

Starrho answered, "There are weapons more powerful on Earth that can turn the world upside down or right side up rather. These weapons are definitely not weapons of violence, force or money, but it is definitely a power far greater."

"Rubbish!" snapped Grodo.

Starrho said, "Look to the Great One, O magician, He can do greater things and give you all you need, but not through violence, not through hatred, not through killing and not through magic. All these earthly weapons of violence will pass away, but in the very end, only the Great One's kingdom will remain."

Grodo glared at them and snarled, "Prepare to go to the worst nightmare, the Prince of Darkness tomorrow, you silly soft-hearted sentimental fools. Good night!"

He walked out mumbling to himself, clearly disturbed. The magic within him could sense a different power from the Star Men and Tara, and even Akim and Sasha, who by now had developed the strength and powers of the Great One. The Star Men were cool, centered, but powerful. There was no turbulence, violence or hate in them, and that disturbed him. Grodo grew up in a world where the motto was "Never forgive, never forget and take revenge."

As he walked out and shut the door after him, they waited for at least twenty minutes before the Star Men, Akim, Tara and Sasha made a circle and held hand singing a queer little song,

> "Today we will fly
> Far, wide and very high
> As night breaks out in the sky
> *We will through forest fly*
> *And our mission will stand*
> *It will never die!"*

As they sang the song, they suddenly all rose together and flew out of the window shooting out like silver arrows.

Some hours later, there was much shouting in the palace as the furious Prince Skotadi found out that they had escaped!

Grodo, the magician was angry with himself, as he did not figure out their escape plan. He found himself hating the Star Men, the boy, the girl and the woman, hating their guts, hating the way they spoke mystically of higher things that he Grodo, the powerful magician knew nothing about. He suddenly felt uncertain and this unsettling feeling unnerved him.

Chapter 15
The Dark Forest and the Battle

As they flew out in the night with the stars ahead, Dendal said, "We should go and meet Dimho, he said he would tell us the way to the forests."

Tara said, "We gotta go very fast, the prince and magician will be on the prowl for us."

The Star Men flew towards Dimho's little house. Dimho was anxiously standing outside his house as if he was waiting for them. As soon as he saw them, he said gladly, "I was so worried about you all when you did not return after your walk, what happened?'

Starrho quickly relayed the events and Dimho's eyes widened in horror and said, "You got to leave immediately to the Dark Forests. Now, just follow the huge city light, an enormous light is on a gigantic statue of a snake. As you come to the giant snake statue, you will see forests some miles away from the city, and fly in that direction. Once you are in the forests, fly high above so none of the forest creatures can attack you. As you keep flying, look out for a cave. When you see a huge cave, look out for the Green Snake, he lives there."

Starrho said gratefully, "Thank you so much Dimho, we will meet you after this is all over, bye!"

Dimho watched them fly up in the air and thought worriedly, *hope they will be safe.*

The Star Men kept looking out for the light, and the Sasha spotted a light and said, "There, I see a light brighter than the others."

Akim agreed, "This must be the light, it is way above in the sky and brighter."

"Good work Sasha," said Dendal, "You have sharp eyes!"

Sasha glowed happily.

Soon, they were flying closer to the light and then they did see the gigantic statue of a snake. When they reached the statue, they looked over the city and from a distance they could see a stretch of forest. They flew over the City of Skilk, thousands of lights glimmering all over, and the blue-gray smoke and noise of the city rose to the air.

The Star Men, Akim, Tara and Sasha flew on the cool current of the wind and rose even higher. As they approached the forest, they saw it was very dense, dark and ugly. The old gnarled trees looked like old angry monsters glaring at them and waved arms menacingly. Sometimes, the arms of the trees reached out to grab them, who were of course higher than the trees. The forest seemed to have black figures floating around menacingly.

"Sing!" said Dendal, "Don't stop singing!"

At first, it was difficult to sing in the thick evil atmosphere of the forest, but slowly, a song finally flew out. They sang gustily trying to sound braver than they felt. As they kept singing, they felt braver and stronger. Eventually, the forest started to be flooded with the powerful song of the Star Men, Akim, Tara and Sasha.

As they flew through the dark forest, they saw more evil ghouls rising up to meet them but with the power of the song, the ghouls started trembling. They hated those songs from the One Above and the ghouls shrieked in the darkness and flew off hurriedly.

"Do not stop!" warned Starrho, "They are many of them and ferocious too!"

They all continued singing. The songs had Light and Truth. The things of the darkness and evil hated it. The forest rose with disturbed resonance and tremors.

Finally, they saw a huge, huge gray cave with a gaping mouth. It reminded them of a very hungry ferocious dragon. As they flew down to the cave, they saw at the entrance, a very gigantic huge Green Snake.

"Great snakes, this must be the biggest snake on Earth!" exclaimed Akim. It was an enormous snake.

Sasha exclaimed, "Yikes, I can't imagine going near the snake!"

"Shhh," said Grinko, "We should not talk much!"

Just then, the Snake looked up and saw them. He swayed a little, and they could see flashes of light coming from the eyes of the snake!

Starrho said quietly to the others, "This looks a very dangerous and intelligent snake, too cunning, so we have to be extra sharp."

Tara said, "As it is said, the Green Snake is hiding the Golden Book, it must be in his cave. There has to be a way that we can get into his cave…How should we do it?"

Piran said, "I have a plan, we have to divert the Snake's attention and one of us has to get inside."
Akim said quickly and urgently, "I just heard an instruction from the Great One that as you divert him I have to run in and get The Golden Book!"

Grinko said worriedly, "Akim, how can we let you in? It will be dangerous!"

Dendal said calmly, "If the Great One has given this instruction to Akim, we have to obey, let Akim go in, but we will try to help him to get out soon."

Piran said, "I play the flute, so I will distract him. As they neared landed on the ground, Piran pulled out a flute playing a beautiful haunting melody. It was not the music from above but earthly music. The Star Men did a little dance along with the music. Tara and Sasha nearly burst out laughing because they looked so comical.

The Green Snake first hissed, while strange light flashed out from his eyes, but despite trying to resist the tune, he started to sway to the music of the flute.

The Green Snake spoke to them saying after a while saying, "Don't take another step further near my cave or I will kill you all with a slash from my tail or a poisonous bite!"

The Green Snake had a raspy whispering hissy kind of voice. Tara and Sasha shuddered when they heard that. The Star Men went on calmly. Piran kept on playing the flute softly and the Star Men continued their little dance before the Green Snake to keep him entertained. Once again, the Green Snake started to get greatly engrossed in the flute music. He kept his eyes fixed on the Star Men.

In the meantime, Akim quietly slipped into the cave. As Akim ran in, he rushed inside a huge dark cave.

It had a damp horrible smell. Akin noticed that in the deep dark corner, he saw a big black stone on top of which was an object covered with a black cloth. Akim went to it and uncovered it and gasped, it was a huge Book. It was no ordinary Book, it glistened and shimmered and in its light, Akim started to feel new great things rising up within him.

He picked it up knowing instantly it was the Golden Book. He thought, "This Book is so powerful that the Green Snake had to cover it, he hates its light!" As he was trying to slip out of the cave silently, the Green Snake suddenly turned around and saw Akim in the cave.

The Green Snake screamed madly, "You think I am a fool you idiot, do you think you can get away from this, now I am going to get you and kill you!"

As the Green Snake slithered towards Akim in a mode of attack, Akim tried to hide behind the big black stone in the corner of the cave. The Green Snake came towards him and Akim again ran to the other end of the cave, still holding on tightly to the Golden Book.

The Green Snake chased Akim and was about to bite Akim with his fangs. Akim tripped and fell to the ground, his heart sinking.

All hope was gone. Akim thought he was about to die just as the Green Snake was about to dig his fangs into Akim's arm. Just then, Billho and Zora suddenly flew in like lightning and snatched up Akim, who was still holding on to the Golden Book tightly.

The Green Snake raised his head trying to catch them, but they flew out too quickly. The other Star Men followed and flew up in the dark night way out of the reach of the maddened Green Snake.

The Green Snake called out in a hissy shrill voice, "Give me that Book or things will go very bad for you!"

"Worry about yourself Green Snake, your time is close to the end!" shouted out Roko.

Then Starrho cried out, "Oh no, Tara and Sasha were left behind, in that hurry, we could not grab them, we got to get them too!"

Just then, the evil forest trees started to wave their arms furiously. The ghouls tried to come down shrieking trying to attack the Star Men and Akim who rose even higher. The Green Snake started to scream out aloud in a hissing kind of scream. He was calling for help.

A few minutes later, an army came trampling in on horses in the forest. It was the Prince of Darkness' army, which was why they could arrive so fast as their horses could run nearly as fast as lightning. They were everywhere, rushing everywhere, with flashing silver weapons that Akim had never seen before.

"Fly up higher," called out Dendal, "And do not stop singing, I can see that Tara and Sasha are hiding in the bushes, we will get them later!"

The King of Darkness' army could not fly, but very soon, the killer vultures and even the Seekers came flying in like a black cloud of fury.

The Star Men took out their silver swords, swinging them in the air.

Akim asked them, "Why do you wave your swords in the air? I have seen you do this in every battle."

Piran replied, "These are swords which slice away the evil works, the malice, the rage, the spirit of murder and kill and hatred. As we slice them in the air, those evil works start to crumble. The Prince of Darkness is the

Prince of the Air, and we fight our battles against the evil things in the air, not with flesh and blood. Our weapons are not earthly weapons. We do not kill the flesh and pour out blood, but our weapons are higher weapons of the Great One, supernatural ones, which destroy evil, and only then will the battle be won!"

"Very interesting," said Akim deeply impressed as he could already see some black things in the air crumbling down, and fade away like mist.

Suddenly they noticed a change in the battlefield below. The killer vultures could not fly close enough to attack the Star Men and Akim. Below, he suddenly noticed that Prince of Darkness's Army was getting scattered all over. There seemed to be a great confusion below. Through all this, the Star Men were singing and waving their swords in the air, slicing down evil works, and that powerful song penetrated the evil in the air, driving it away!

Then, to their great horror, they noticed it was Tara and Sasha had come out from the bushes.

Wise Dendal said calmly, "There is always a reason for everything, they are not foolish or impulsive, and they must have come out for a purpose."

The raging Army did not seem to notice Tara and Sasha, which was a good thing. They were standing in the forest somewhere near some tall trees. The Army was moving around in confusion, aware that the Star Men and Akim were now up a little higher than the trees. The Seekers and vultures did not dare to come near the Star Men and Akim as the evil things were fading into wisps of mist.

In the meantime, the situation had changed for the Star Men and Akim. They knew they could not abandon

Tara and Sasha, so they waited, Akim holding the Golden Book, which glowed in the dark.

"I understand why the Green Snake covered the Golden Book with a cloth." said Akim, "He could not bear the light of the Golden Book."

"Yes, they hate the Light, they belong to the Prince of Darkness, Light and Darkness never mix, but remember, the Light always floods and displaces the Darkness," said Starrho.

"We have to do something," said Zora urgently, "or they will attack Tara and Sasha when they notice them."

Suddenly they noticed Prince Skotadi among the Army and worse still the Magician, Grodo, with his magical powers!

Akim groaned, "We could not have it worse, it is worse than we thought!"

"Sing, sing, sing" said Starrho, "These are our weapons, we do not kill, we do not fight with violence."

They made a circle above the raging army below them and the Army below was aiming arrows at them. The arrows always missed the Star Men and Akim. The Star Men sang a powerful song that sounded eerie to the Army below. This song was empowered by the Great One. The song went like this:

"When Darkness floods
Then Light over floods
Darkness will be shattered tonight
As we fight the Great One's fight
And then the Earth will shine
With the Great One's Light
The Golden Book will be read again

> *And Love and Truth*
> *Will reign!"*

As they continued to sing, the Army and all belonging to the Kingdom of Darkness started to tremble like jelly. They could not stop. They did not understand it was the power of the Great One.

Prince Skotadi looked up waving his fist and shouted in his loud rambunctious manner, "Your silly songs are weak and idiotic and we will destroy you in the end!"

After he said this, it started to thunder, lightning flashed and there was a downpour of heavy rain.

A strange confusion started erupting with the Army below. They started to scatter further as if they lost all sense of direction. They could not aim their arrows any more at the Star Men and Akim. Then another puzzling phenomenon started to happen. The Army started attacking each other in their confusion!

A great fight rose up among them and in that angry bantering, Grodo the Magician seemed to stand in a trance, affixed, as if he could not do anything. They heard the Prince Skotadi shouting, "Grodo, do something fast!" but Grodo stood in a trance.

The storm grew in intensity. Then another incongruous occurrence happened. Suddenly, the trees around them started to fall down in the storm, mysteriously so because it was not the force of the rain causing them to fall, but another force. Trees came crashing down, causing panic and then the inevitable happened; the Army started fleeing away as fast as they could!

In the meantime, they saw the Green Snake hissing furiously and slithering on the ground. The Green Snake had suddenly noticed Tara and Sasha. He kept looking at Tara and slithering towards her and when he was about to reach her, he raised his head looking as if he was about to strike her. Tara stood calmly and did not move or react. Before anyone could do anything to help her, something stunning happened; a huge gigantic tree came crashing down and fell directly on the Green Snake, missing Tara by inches. That enormous tree hit hard on the Green Snake crushing his head! Without raising a single weapon being raised, the Green Snake lay dead!

Prince Skotadi saw this, gave a howl of fury and rage and aimed his arrow to shoot Tara.

Then, something unexpected happened, Grodo the Magician came from behind and stopped Prince Skotadi with a command saying, "No, leave them alone, if you touch them, greater harm will come upon you. I prophecy to you Prince Skotadi that you leave immediately from the City of Skilk and live a simple life elsewhere or you will die!"

Prince Skotadi was furious to hear this. Grodo the Magician was speaking to him with an authority he had never seen before.

He glared at Grodo and yelled, "Get out you nincompoop and help me to fight and kill these evil people, they are destroying my kingdom!"

Grodo replied, "Prince Skotadi, if you do anything now, it will be worse for you; right now things are not in your favor!"

On hearing this, Prince Skotadi panicked. He knew Grodo was always right.

He said to Grodo, "Grodo, I am surprised at you. I thought with your magic, you would defeat them!"

Grodo replied, "They have something with them that is blocking my magic, I do not know what it is, but my magic is not working!"

Prince Skotadi yelled at the Star Men and others, "You evil creatures, you destructive elements, you will pay heavily for this!"

The Star Men landed on the ground next to Prince Skotadi and looked at him evenly while Starrho replied calmly, "We have not touched anyone or killed anyone. It is the violence in your own hearts that is destroying yourselves, turn away from evil while there is still time."

Prince Skotadi snorted scornfully and said, "I have power and wealth like no one else has, I will rule the world one day, I have more success than you!"

Dental said, "We do not look for Earthly success, it fades away too, like that black mist you saw evaporating!"

Prince Skotadi had nothing to say, but somehow saw the truth in those words as the Star Men and the others had not raised a weapon against The Prince of Darkness Army or Prince Skotadi's Army. The Seekers, the Prince of Darkness Army, and the vultures were trying to fight against the Star Men and Akim, and yet all were being destroyed or fleeing!

Prince Skotadi with his clothes dripping heavily with rain sputtered at the Star Men angrily screamed, "Your days are numbered!"

He watched the trees falling around the forest nervously, the violet storm raged and his soldiers were fleeing away fast. He looked at Grodo and said shortly and rudely, "I will see you later at the palace, Grodo, meet me there in the morning." With that, he leaped unto his black stallion and raced away as fast as he could towards the palace.

With the trees falling, it seemed that the strange song had its effect on the trees where the ghouls and evil spirits lived as they all shivered in fear on hearing the strange song of the Star Men.

Tara and Sasha came up and joined the Star Men and Akim.

Tara said smiling, "One thing good is that the Green Snake is dead. If he were alive, he would cause greater damage on the Earth. Now is the time for a new awakening on the Earth…the season of singing is about to arrive!"

Everyone felt exhilarating joy as Tara said that as if a powerful wonderful new thing was about to happen.

Chapter 16
Grodo the Magician

The storm became even more brutal and wild although the trees had stopped crashing down and in the pelting pouring rain, everyone ran under the trees. Lightning flashed and thunder crashed.

The ghouls were mysteriously silence or were afraid to attack because they were terrified of the groaning falling trees. The sudden death of the great Green Snake perplexed them and frightened them. It seemed to them as if their protection was gone.

Everyone drenched wet, was standing under an enormous old banyan tree in whipping lashing rain as blue-purple lightning ripping the sky. Starrho said triumphantly, "See how all the bad things were scattered and destroyed without using violence, this can only happen when WE walk in pure Light!"

Akim said happily, "And we got the Golden Book, what a victory, I can feel the power coming from the Book, which was why the Green Snake hid the Book and covered it, he could not bear to look at it!"

Tara said admiringly, "You were so brave and fearless, Akim, we are so proud of you, you accomplished the mission, the Great One is so pleased!"
Akim glowed feeling warm and was about to speak. Just then, everyone suddenly got a nasty shock and Sasha exclaimed, "Oh no, the magician!" They all suddenly noticed Grodo the Magician standing near the banyan tree watching them silently!

Then Grodo walked slowly towards them. Akim and Sasha were uneasy, and the Star Men watched him silently and Tara looked at him fearlessly. They somehow sensed this moment was a defining moment.

Grodo came up to them and said calmly and quietly to them, "My name is Grodo the Magician. We have met before as you know, once in the dwarf's cottage in the mountains, and once again in Prince Skotadi's palace.

Starrho said politely, "Pleased to formally meet you Grodo!"

Grodo said, "Though I am a magician with great powers, you all have something, which I do not, even with my magic. You have a deep peace, calm, and you seem to know beyond the beyond. I can tell the future, but I cannot tell beyond the beyond. I have grown up in a culture of hate that says never forgive, never forget and take revenge. You do not have revenge in you at all, but still you are victorious, even if we kill you, you will still win, and we have lost!"

Tara answered Grodo gently, "We look above, and walk step by step, and our gifts, strength and blessings come from Great One. We live in hope, we live in love, we live in joy, and we get strength. Hatred is not our driving force. If we hate, we have lost the war. Hatred belongs to the Prince of Darkness. Love belongs to the Great One. Grodo, look to the Great One and not within yourself, look up and your joy will be full!"

Grodo shook his head and looked away. For the first time in his life, he felt at a loss and he was not sure what to do. To follow the Great One seemed a weak thing to do. At the same time, he was grateful that none of them rebuked him or scorned him for coming to them at this moment at his weak moment. Grodo did not realize that in reality, it was his strongest moment. In displaying his vulnerability in humility, it was strength because with humility comes great strength and courage.

Tara continued "Talk to Him, Grodo, talk to Him and remember, once you go to the Great One, you cannot practice magic again. It is against the Great One's wish that anyone should practice magic. Magic opens doors to evil spirits that harm a person. Magic gives temporary power gain and fame, but in the end, we are separated from the Great One. One can never go to the Golden Land if they practice magic. Are you willing Grodo?"

Grodo thought for a long time, and then went to sit on a smooth rock near the Green Snake's cave. After a long time of thinking, he looked up at all of them and said slowly and thoughtfully, "I have suffered long enough with emptiness in my heart, even with my great magic. Perhaps, I am willing to give up my magic and follow the Great One!"

Everyone was delighted that Grodo, the great magician had made such a choice and made a circle around him singing a beautiful song. Grodo spoke from his heart to the Great One. As Grodo did so, bliss filled his soul and he knew he was different. He raised his voice and started to sing as never before! Grodo started to look different. His face was calmer and kinder, though he still had the grandness around him.

It was a wonderful moment for all. Then suddenly they realized they were all drenching wet and cold and needed to get warm and dry again and Akim suddenly thought of hot tea and buttered toast.

Tara said, "Come along, we need to dry and warm ourselves, but where shall we go."

The Star Men could not fly far now, because of the stormy weather and they could only fly high above the trees and stay there.

Grodo told them all, "We'll go to my family house, I rarely live there, I mostly live in the palace, but there is a young man, a good friend who lives there, come along on my horses, I have six beautiful stallions!"

They all climbed on the huge grand gleaming horses that raced through the Dark Forests. The ghouls and spirits shrieked out at them rudely, but did not dare to attack them.

It was very eerie riding back through the Dark Forests with the wild animals howling. Finally, they came to the edge of the forest, and to the City of Skilk. Grodo led them through the city and they finally made their way back to a huge house to which Grodo took them. There was a young man, who was living in the house.

His eyes lit up when he saw Grodo and the company and exclaimed, "Grodo, you are back after a long time, I thought you were in a battle with Prince Skotadi as rumors told me!"

Grodo said, "Jojo, I have left the company of Prince Skotadi, and Prince Skotadi left the battle. Now here are the people we were battling, but guess what, in the end we became friends!"

Jojo's eyes widened in amazement and said, "Before you speak further, you all need a hot bath and a good meal and then we'll talk!"

He immediately lit up a fire to heat water, so they could have hot-water baths in the cold stormy weather. He gave them new sets of fresh clothes and later served them all a very palatable dinner.

Grodo told the others, "Jojo is one of my most faithful friends, I never used to live here, but in the palace, but Jojo stays here and has been staying here since ten years old when he lost his parents and my parents, who died, brought Jojo home. Now, whenever I needed a break, I would come and hang out here with Jojo."

Everyone liked Jojo. Jojo seemed a kind-hearted person, and very soon, Grodo was telling Jojo all what happened, including Prince Skotadi's army getting defeated. He even told him about the Golden Book and about his understanding of the Great One and how wonderful He was!

As Jojo listened in amazement, he said, "I too want to follow the Great One. I am tired of all the evil around in the City of Skilk."

Grodo said, "I think both Jojo and I want to get out of the City of Skilk, can we come where you are going?" he asked no one in particular.

Tara answered, "You could have come, but Grodo, you are to be the new king in the City of Skilk!"

Grodo along with everyone else looked flabbergasted. Grodo shook his head saying, "I cannot just take over as king and Prince Skotadi will kill me anyway. There will be anarchy in the kingdom!"

Tara looked very majestic at that moment with her skin glowing and eyes shining as she looked at Grodo earnestly and said, "There are many in the city that need your help Grodo. The City of Skilk has no one. If you do not rule, the city will go into greater darkness. Prince Skotadi is not the one to rule. He is an evil dictator. A dictator will always ruin a country. Prince Skotadi said he would be at the palace, but you want to know the truth, he has deserted his kingdom and run away!"

Grodo shook his head and said, "The people here are not good, even if there was a good ruler, I am sure they will kill him or me!"

Dendal replied, "We cannot judge anything or anyone so quickly. When given a chance, people do change many times. Better circumstances sometimes can help people to become better people. People sometimes need the benefit of a doubt. Do give it to them, Grodo!"

As Grodo sat for a long time again thinking, he suddenly said, "I surrender!"

"What do you mean by surrender, surrender to Prince Skotadi?" asked Akim a little horrified.

"No, no!" said Grodo smiling, "I did not mean that, how could I, not after all that I have experienced in knowing the Great One."

Tara explained to Akim, "Surrender is to yield, let go of everything, release it, and die to it and to your desires. Then you will be free. Self-life is ego and ego is a stumbling block."

Tara went on to sing a song softly....

"When Self Life is strong

The Big I thrives on
Ego is a big ugly stone
It slows down and obstructs
It keeps all doors locked
Surrender is a flow
Bringing change
Wherever it goes
It has an unseen power
That no one seems to know"
Miracles always happen
With the Power of Surrender!"

Grodo was slowly starting to understand this new life.

Grodo said, "I will rule, but I need men from the kingdom to join as it will be a tough battle. Can you stay and help me too?"

The others agreed to stand with Grodo until he became king because they realized many hoodlums could provoke trouble in the City of Skilk.

Starrho added, "Another thing King Grodo, wherever you go, you will find people are about the same. In the City of Skilk, you saw that selfishness. Now, if you go to a little town, you might see the same. What really changes people is Truth and Light that pours into their hearts to change them from within!"

Grodo nodded, but he was a little worried as he could no longer rely on his magic and would be defeated. Starrho seemed to read Grodo's mind and said, "Grodo, do not fear Prince Skotadi. The Great One protects you now, He will take care of you and no harm will come to you!"

Grodo nodded again feeling helpless without his magic. However, that night as he went to bed and closed his eyes, in the cool quiet darkness, he realized he was far richer and happier inside now. The vacuum in his soul overflowed with warmth and he had a strange love for people he never had before.

He felt that the Golden Book, which Akim had with him, was a living book. It was alive!

Tara had told them they would all get copies from the original Golden Book. Grodo was looking forward for his own copy of the Golden Book so he could understand more and get internal strength. When Grodo finally fell asleep, he had a happy smile on his face!

Chapter 17
Prince Skotadi

The next day was an extremely busy one with a flurry of activities. Grodo and Jojo rapidly packed some belongings, and walked toward the palace along with the Star Men, Tara, Akim and Sasha.

The streets looked deserted. A few people on the streets stared at them, some whispered, and others quickly walked away. They were afraid to speak to Grodo and they were afraid of the strange looking tall shining men company of men that Grodo was with, the boy, girl and the beautiful woman who they feared was a witch.

Dimho caught sight of them and ran up to them crying, "Hello, hello! So happy you made it back safe, I was worried. All the people in the City of Skilk are talking about the battle. They are saying that Prince Skotadi's was defeated and the Army has disappeared.

The rumor has spread around of you, the Star Men and news is buzzing in the air that the city will be ruled by strange aliens and everyone is afraid." Dimho suddenly noticed Grodo and gave a start.

Starrho said smoothly, "Dimho, meet the new Grodo, he is no longer a magician, but going to be the new king in the City of Skilk!"

Dimho looked very surprised and said softly almost shyly to Grodo, "Long live the King!"

Dimho accompanied them on the walk down to the palace as the others started to tell Dimho what happened in the Dark Forest and about the battle and Dimho listened wide-eyed and fascinated. As they entered the palace, it looked empty. No guards were around, and they found some guards sleeping in the huge gardens! Many of the guards and Army had fled overseas because they were afraid to face the wrath of Prince Skotadi.

Grodo had expected to find Prince Skotadi in the palace but did not find him anywhere. He finally asked a half asleep guard where Prince Skotadi was and the guard got up with a start, looked at Grodo through half-open eyes, and said "Eh!" and went back to sleep snoring loudly.

Grodo did know whether to be angry or amused, but when he heard the Star Men, Akim, Tara and Sasha chuckling in the background, he smiled along thinking, "Before, if such a thing happened, I would have thrown them to the sharks with the full approval of Prince Skotadi!"

A soldier came up to Grodo and said, "I was one of the soldiers fighting in the Army last night and had seen Prince Skotadi racing back to the palace in the night, and then left last night!"

Grodo replied, "I do know that Prince Skotadi had fled from the battlegrounds, but he said he was going to the palace!"

Slowly, the other guards and palace attendants started to awaken. They all knew that Prince Skotadi had left with some luggage on his favorite horse, but they had no idea where he went. In fact, they were all relieved he had gone and were secretly hoping he would not come back!

It was not very long before many of the palace folks had gotten to know that Grodo would be their new king. In fact, the Star Men declared solemnly, "King Grodo will be a good king, and give justice to the people of the City of Skilk, he is chosen by the Great One Himself. Prince Skotadi has fled. His rule of dictatorship will bring anarchy and chaos to the people."

The palace folk were all in awe of the glowing Star Men who said Grodo would be a good ruler, chosen by the Great One. The palace people of course had no idea who The Great One was. They thought He was another king from another country!

Soon the news traveled fast though the City of Skilk that Prince Skotadi had fled and Grodo would be the new king!

Many of the people welcomed Grodo as the new king as they looked up to Grodo for his wisdom and knew he was a great magician, although they did not know that Grodo was going to stop using his magic.

Even though Prince Skotadi had disappeared, everyone was uncomfortable, not knowing if he would return and cause a lot of trouble.

The cooks in the palace had cooked a delicious meal and the helpers in the palace called King Grodo, the Star Men and the others to eat. They went into a huge beautiful room, which had a huge table laden with delicious food.

Sasha exclaimed, "I'm starving, and the food looks delicious, unlike anything I have ever seen!"

Akim agreed and said, "I'm glad the helpers in the palace thought about food, I was starting to feel very hungry.

They all sat at the table and were about to eat when they heard a chilling hard voice behind them.

"You have come to MY palace, sitting at MY table and eating MY food. You are a terrible traitor Grodo; I never thought this of you. I got news from Kow, my head vulture that you declared yourself the new king, this is treachery!"

They turned to see Prince Skotadi standing, dressed in black, his eyes coal black and hard. Even the Star Men shivered when looking at him.

Grodo looked at him calmly not afraid. He suddenly felt a newfound courage that he never ever had before and said gently, "Prince Skotadi, you never wanted the good of the people in the City of Skilk. You allowed the rich to become too rich, the intermediary to be always struggling, and the poor to be always hungry and weak.

Prince Skotadi growled, "It is a lie! I brought prosperity to all!"

Grodo shook his head and said, "You knew if the City of Skilk grew to be prosperous and powerful, it would limit your control over the city. You controlled people by making them dependent on you and not giving them freedom. The truth is you are not the destined ruler for the kingdom. I am not taking over by treachery, but it is destiny that I must fulfill given to me by The Great One!"

At the mention of The Great One, Prince Skotadi started to spurt out unmentionable profanities and prance around like an angry bull.

Everyone was alarmed except for Grodo who was accustomed to Prince Skotadi's ranting and raving.

Grodo softened on looking at his old angry friend, "Calm down Prince Skotadi. If you promise to change, you can rule the south part of the city." Grodo said it because he started to feel sorry for Prince Skotadi.

Tara shook her head and said firmly, "No, it cannot be so, for Prince Skotadi has no change in heart, he belongs to the Darkness by his choice, some do not change."

Prince Skotadi glared at Tara and said disdainfully, "Silly interfering woman, what do you know? Go and wash your pots and pans in the kitchen! Have you ever ruled a kingdom? Do you know about great rulers, the things they go through and the great battles they fight? Go back to the gutter from where you came from!"

Tara did not react, but stood quietly watching Prince Skotadi. Suddenly Prince Skotadi came in front of Grodo and he swiftly drew out something from a pocket, a small sharp silver dagger and to the horror of everyone, was about to thrust it into Grodo's heart. However, Grodo managed to duck just in time. In the meantime, the Star Men, as swift as they were all flew and caught Prince Skotadi and managed to throw the dagger out of his hand.

When Prince Skotadi found he was helpless, he first gave a yell of frustration. Then after a few moments, he abruptly changed and said in a friendly tone to Grodo, "Now Grodo, I am sorry for that little outburst, I am under a lot of stress, forgive me my man. Have you forgotten all the wonderful times we had together? How can you leave me now for some strangers you never knew before? Come on, let us go to the marble balcony and talk things out. Perhaps we can work out a deal. You say the Great One has chosen you, well I will not argue about that, but perhaps we can still work together in ruling."

"Don't go," warned Tara, but Grodo paid no heed as at that moment, his emotions got the better of him. He started remembering the good times he had with Prince Skotadi. Grodo was also feeling guilty, as he was actually usurping Prince Skotadi's throne. He suddenly wished that this responsibility of being king were never his.

They both went to the balcony, which had a magnificent view of the gardens. A thick ledge surrounded the balcony. Prince Skotadi and Grodo in the old days would sit on the ledge discussing all their plans when the moon was full; or Grodo would practice his magic there. As Prince Skotadi sat on the ledge, he invited Grodo to come and sit along beside him.

Starrho told the others, "Come on along, don't leave them alone."

Prince Skotadi saw them coming to the balcony and growled at them saying "Can't you leave two old friends alone, you interfering lot, go!"

Prince Skotadi turned to Grodo and said, "Okay Grodo, you win, I understand I was evil and wrong and I wish to change, I accept your offer to give me the south part of the city to rule."

Grodo answered, "I am so glad for the change of heart."

Then, at the next moment, Prince Skotadi pushed a very shocked Grodo off the ledge! Zora the Star Man whose reflexes were very quick flew and caught Grodo and pulled him up. Prince Skotadi kept trying to push Grodo down off the ledge and in that scuffle and struggle Prince Skotadi suddenly slipped and fell down. All the people in the palace grounds saw Prince Skotadi hurtling down and hitting the concrete grounds below the balcony. People gazed at Prince Skotadi petrified.

Grodo was shocked to see Prince Skotadi lying below. His heart was very sad even though Prince Skotadi tried to kill him. In fact, Grodo forgave Prince Skotadi for trying to kill him at that very moment. Something new and forgiving arose in Grodo's heart.

As everyone rushed to Prince Skotadi, they found that he was still breathing and Grodo shouted from the balcony, "If he is still breathing and not dead, take him to the hospital!"

The soldier below shouted back, "Wouldn't it be better to let him die, O King Grodo? After all, he wanted to kill you!"

Grodo shook his head and ordered, "Take him to the hospital!"

Many of the people did not want Prince Skotadi to get any help at all. Soon, they gathered people and started marching on the streets chanting with banners written, "A DICTATOR SHOULD DIE!"

Grodo did not agree. He said, "I forgive him because he does not know what he is doing."

"Leave Grodo alone," said Dendal to the others, "Kindness is bound in the heart of the greatest kings. Grodo will be a very noble king!"

They took Prince Skotadi to the hospital. The next few hours were very serious and grave. The doctors declared that he would barely be able to survive the night and the citizens of the City of Skilk were all hoping that he would die!

Starrho said to the others, "When a dictator rules, petrified people pretend to love him, but when he dies, people openly rejoice!"
Akim said, "We have seen this happen before our eyes!"

The rest of the day flew in a stream of events with Grodo and others writing petitions and letters to different leaders in the government. That evening, the coronation ceremony for Grodo was to take place. Starrho advised, "There should be no delay in the coronation and it should be done as quickly as possible." Everone agreed. No one objected to Grodo being the new king. No one could think of anyone better than Grodo.

Akim then said wistfully, "Now all the adventures are nearly over…everyone played a great part. I sometimes feel my mission was nothing important, anyone could have done what I did!"

Starrho eyes twinkled and said, "A little star can light up the dark! Akim, you did something very important in that moment of time. You picked up the Golden Book and rescued it out of the cave very boldly and successfully. I now give you another task. You have to make copies and share the Golden Book on the Earth with all the people on the Earth. The Great One knows of your faithfulness to finish things. Everything you did in your life was faithful even when no one was watching. Now, you are openly rewarded. Your little light in the dark will soon become a great light!"

Akim smiled and said, "I am not looking for glory, but I am happy that the Great One thinks I am worthy. I cannot wait for the coronation of King Grodo, it is so exciting!"

Starrho then said something that surprised everyone "Something important has to be done before the coronation of King Grodo."

"What?" asked everyone wondering what in the world could it be.

Chapter 18
The Iron Ball, the Light, and the Ship Journey

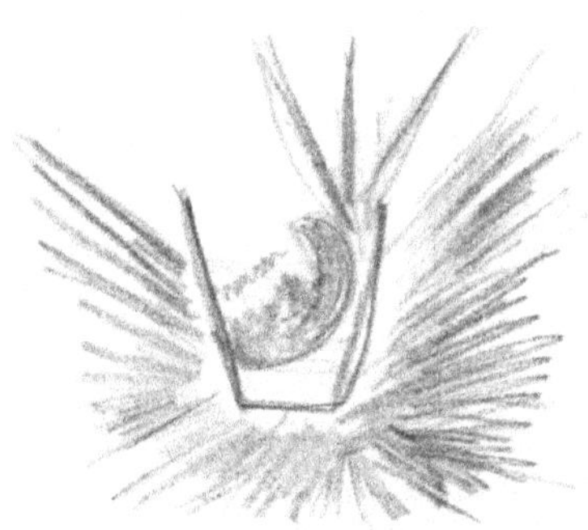

Starrho told everyone quietly, "We'll have to make thousands of copies of the Golden Book and give it to whoever will take it."

Grodo interrupted, "Something important has to be done before that."
"What?" asked everyone almost together even more mystified thinking things were getting more and more complicated.

"Very important," continued Grodo, "We have to find the iron ball which has enclosed the Golden Light. This light is very important. It floods the Earth and opens the minds of people to understand. When they start to understand, they will stop hating, fighting, killing, because the Light of Truth will come inside them."

"Where can we find it?" asked Tara.
Grodo replied, "It's in the palace itself. Prince Skotadi hated it and he kept entrapped in the iron ball, I think he kept it somewhere in his bedroom chambers. Let's go there."

They went through the palace and eventually came to the grand beautiful chambers of Prince Skotadi and searched the room. Suddenly Sasha noticed a very beautiful picture that looked almost alive. It had a silver river with soft powdery sand in the banks. She reached out and touched it the sand, and sprang back very surprised!

"I think the iron ball is somewhere in the picture!" she said excitedly not exactly knowing why she said that.

Everyone looked hard and Grodo touched the picture slowly, as he did so, he felt a tracing of lines with his fingers, which he followed. He eventually found a spot in the picture on the powdery sand where there was an iron pot. He pressed it hard and everyone got a shock. Out of the picture popped out a huge iron ball, black as the night. It flew out and sat on the floor! They all stared at it, afraid, as it looked grim and forbidding.

Then Grodo cleared his throat and said, "Now, another task, we have to find the glass of blue water, Prince Skotadi always kept it hidden somewhere. Only the blue water can dissolve the iron ball!"

Billho groaned and said, "Isn't this complicated!" Dendal said, "Remember dear Billho, it is a step-by-step journey, we need a lot of patience along the way...but in the end, it will be all worth it!"

Billho replied, "As always, you are right, dear wise Dendal! I agree!"
They carefully searched the whole palace looking for the glass of blue water, but could not find a trace of it.

"Do you think Prince Skotadi threw it away?" asked Sasha, "I wonder how we can possibly find the glass of blue water."
Grodo shook his head and said, "No, if he threw it away, he would come under a curse himself, it was very

important for him to preserve that water, so he just hid it, he was always afraid to throw it even though he hated it."

They kept searching for a long time and then Grodo suddenly remembered a room that Prince Skotadi always kept locked.

He had no idea where the keys were, so they voted to break down the door and with the help of some guards was able to break down the heavy wooden teak door. As they went inside, they immediately saw a table and on it, a crystal glass filled with clear sparkling blue water. They picked it up, ran to Prince Skotadi's bedroom chambers, immersed the black iron ball into the crystal glass of blue water, and started singing a song:

"Iron ball
We break your curse
Release the Golden Light
Truth, Light and Love
Will now rule with might!"

As they sang this song, the iron ball in the sparkling blue water started to rumble and crack, and finally split open in half. A sizzling pure golden light flooded the room. It was not blinding, but beautiful. It slowly began to flow all over, and streamed out of the room. To their astonishment, they saw the golden hue of light almost covering as far as their eyes could see, covering the Earth like a canopy. It looked very breathtaking.

The people walking on the streets of the City of Skilk felt the warmth and beauty of the Golden Light around them and started to feel very calm and peaceful. A sort of glory hung on the Earth!

Starrho said softly, "This Light is shown to you all temporarily. It will fade away. People have to read the Golden Book and then the fullness of the Golden Light will enter their understanding. That glory and Light will fade away if the people do not read the Book and practice its Truth."

Piran added, "The Golden Light gives understanding to the Truth of the Golden Book and in practicing the Truth, it releases its power in the people who practice it, and this Truth keeps spreading, it never remains stagnant in one place!"

Akim said wonderingly, "It sounds so fascinating, I just can't wait to get back to Dora Valley and share this with the folks there!"

"Now," said Starrho, "We will make copies of the Golden Book and put them in stalls everywhere starting with the City of Skilk because NOW the Golden Light is released all over the Earth. This is the Era of Understanding and Truth."

The coronation took place that the evening and the whole City of Skilk was invited for this impressive grand event. Multitudes of people thronged far beyond the palace grounds. Important dignitaries and government leaders attended the coronation. The Star Men and Tara coroneted and anointed Grodo with power, authority, wisdom and the kindness of a real king. He was now King Grodo. Everyone cheered loudly after the coronation. Then, a fantastic dinner held for all in the city where thousands of tables with white-colored tablecloths were placed in rows, and delicious food piled the tables. Multitudes ate the most sumptuous dinner while beautiful music drifted all over the city. There never was a happier day in the City of Skilk. Later, multicolored hues of fireworks lit up the entire city. Tiny colored glowing pretty lights hung all over the city in trees, lampposts and over all the shops. The City of Skilk was sparkling that night.

"Amazing, amazing," exclaimed the citizens of Skilk, "We never saw such wonderful days when Skotadi was there. Now, the best days are ahead of us!"

They did not even call him prince anymore! After this great event, the Star Men, Tara, Akim and Sasha took the Golden Book and placed it on the palace grounds and they again made a circle around the Golden Book and said:

"Multiply O Golden Book. So millions will get the Truth"

Then to the wonder of all present, thousands upon thousands of golden books arose from the original Golden Book. They rose in the air and then softly landed next to the original Golden Book. A faint glow came out of the books, though not as radiant and golden as the original Golden Book.

It was an awesome sight. King Grodo and the others watched stunned. After that, literally, everyone in the City of Skilk picked up the amazing copies of the Golden Books and thousands upon thousands of the city inhabitants started to read the golden books.

All the people in the city were tired of the robberies, murders, corruption and evil that was stalking the streets of the City of Skilk and they wanted truth, love, and mercy to empower their lives in a new way.

As they started to read the books, it seemed that a golden light had pierced their minds and entered into their souls. They got great joy as they read the book and found deep strength to obey the book and do good deeds. It seemed the confusion and chaos was leaving the city.

People stopped fighting, cheating and hating each other. The city began to change and people were happier, there were no more beggars and poverty because the corruption had stopped. The book was teaching them to do the right things and the Golden Light kept entering their hearts to change them. The people became more creative and inventive, and everything started to change in the city.

King Grodo then solemnly declared, "I now give a new name to the City of Skilk, the new name is to be called the City of Netzah, which means city of victory, grace and endurance!"

Everyone clapped their hands. They were happy with the new name as all wanted change; even change of the name of the city was very welcome because the old name was associated with corruption, crime and hatred.

After a couple of days, late in the night, the Star Men, Akim, Tara, and Sasha said their goodbyes to King Grodo and Jojo and all the others. They had to go back soon as they had a lot of work to be done with the original Golden Book.

As the Seven Star Men, Tara, Akim and Sasha returned to the harbor, they got a wonderful surprise. King Asa, Bravo and the other sailors were waiting for them in a beautiful huge white and silver ship!

"Hurrah," shouted Akim joyously.
King Asa smiled at them and said, "You can't trust this weather, sometimes storms will hit and I know the Star Men cannot fly in the storms, so we decided to come and take you back!"

Everyone soon settled in the ship, the ship was sailing over the smooth waters. Days and nights ran on, sometimes choppy and stormy and other times clear and beautiful.

One night as they were all sitting on the deck of the ship, million silver stars sparkling in the sky, the sea was clear and smooth, and they sat together talking through the night.

King Asa told them, "We'll all accompany you Akim to Dora Valley, after which we will take Sasha to her home and then Tara to her home. We will also help you to make copies of the Golden Book… to spread throughout the Earth. We have many helpers in the Island of Tipukut."

"Thank you King Asa," said Akim gratefully. He was very glad for all the help as he was beginning to wonder how he would be able to share the copies with the people of the Earth. His old silly fears had started creeping back, but he shook them away just in time!

He realized teamwork made things happen in a more rewarding and faster way. They all needed each other in some way. He remembered an old saying, "No man is an island and no man stands alone!"

Starrho said, "We will have to go back beyond the stars after we go with you all to Dora Valley."

"Oh no!" exclaimed Akim, "Do you have to go back? Please, please stay with us in Dora Valley, there is so much do; don't go back!"
Starrho replied gravely and kindly, "We are assigned on different missions by the Great One. I do hope on the next mission we will be sent to Earth so we can meet again!"

Everyone looked despondent when they heard this and became suddenly very silent. They realized that there was a chance they would never meet the Star Men again.

Then Dendal said cheerfully, "Cheer up everyone, don't look so sad. There is one day when we will all definitely meet, and that is in the New Kingdom the Great One will make on Earth!"

"Never heard about that," said everyone surprised. "Well," said Dendal, "Let me tell you a little about the beginning of the Earth and the end of Earth."
"End of Earth!" exclaimed Sasha shocked.

Dendal continued as if Sasha did not interrupt, he said, "In the beginning, when the Earth was made, everything was perfect. There was no evil. Then one day, the Prince of Darkness sent a messenger to the people of Earth to deceive the people.

With the lies told to them, the people stopped believing the Great One and evil entered the Earth, death and corruption ruled the Earth. The Great One was sad. He knew that people did wrong things all the time, and they could not enter the Golden Land one day.

Sasha asked, "Why are people now so evil and they do not believe in the Great One anymore?"

Dendal replied, "Over the years, many did not care about right and wrong and never cared what would happen to them in the end. During this time, someone stole the Golden Book. Today, it is found and waiting to be shared again. Now, as copies of the Golden Book will be given to all whomever wants it, the Golden Light will shine on the heart of the people, and the Earth will grow with understanding, wisdom, and love.

As this wonderful time increases over the Earth, a third phase arises. The evil one will rise up again with his destructive army in jealousy. He will rise up ranks to make everyone worship him alone. If they do not, he will want to kill them!

Before he does that, the Great One will send down huge mighty clouds, but these are not normal clouds, these clouds will whisk all the people who love the Great One off the face of the Earth so they will not suffer the terrors that will befall on Earth, such terrors as the Earth has never seen before."

As Dendal said this, everyone shivered; they could almost sense a dread that would one day hit the Earth.

Dendal continued, "The good thing is that all who follow the Great One and obey the Golden Book will escape these horrors. They will be whisked away to the Golden Land. This place is beautiful, glowing, filled with peace, joy and love floods the air and the people are the happiest you can find anyway. We, the Star Men, among other glorious beings with wings will all live there, until the creation of the New Earth.

As he said this, everyone was suddenly flooded with great delight.

Dendal continued. "Meantime, there will be great horrors happening on Earth as never before. In the midst of that great evil, some people will start to believe in the Great One and will want to read the Golden Book. Many of them will run to the mountain caves and hide there. They will remain hidden. The Great One will help them to hide, but sadly some will be found and killed by the Prince of Darkness' people.

"Will you not also help them to escape, Star Men?" asked Akim.

Dendal said, "No, at that great evil tide, we are not sent down, but the Great One will help them to hide, but afterwards, the Winged Warriors will come down and fight this battle against the Prince of Darkness and his evil ones. Finally, in this last battle, as it is known the evil one and his followers will finally be destroyed. Then the New Earth will be made, and we will all come down to live in it!"

Everyone was silent, breathlessly amazed. It sounded too fantastic to be true, but they knew that it would happen, which was why it was so frightening and at the same time, marvelous.

They sat watching the dark sparkling ocean as they sailed on and after a long night, King Asa, Akim, Bravo, Sasha, went down to their cabins still fascinated by the event that Dendal had relayed to them, wondering how it would happen.

Akim said to Bravo, "It sounds very frightening, more frightening than our journeys with the witch and Prince Skotadi and even the Seekers. We had the Star Men with us, but in those days, the Star Men will not come to Earth.

Bravo said, "Well, Dendal did mention the Winged Warriors, now that sounds like big help!"

Akim agreed and said, "The Winged Warriors sound very powerful and a bit scary too."

Sasha said, "Well, if the wickedness is great on Earth at that time, then the Great One will be sending the Winged Warriors, they really sound so exciting, but I am glad we will not be on Earth at that time, things will get so bad!"

Talking and discussing things, the children finally fell asleep.

In the meantime, the Star Men and the sailors stayed awake. Tara still sat on the deck watching the stars and thinking....

The days and weeks rolled by and after a month, they finally arrived in the shores of the Zorran Sea.

As they were arriving towards to shores, King Asa said, "Now, we will have horses with caravans to go to Dora Valley."

Akim said gladly, "I always wanted to travel in a caravan and now I got my wish!"

They finally arrived as they got off the ship, they saw grand caravans with awesome stallions, they were spellbound for a moment!

"Wow!" exclaimed Sasha, "What pretty caravans with such beautiful grand horses!"

King Asa said smiling, "We need to go across rough mountain roads, and I thought the horses would do it best!"

They all had a nice hot breakfast given by King Asa's men who had brought baskets of food and gave everyone cups of refreshing steaming hot tea. They all ate at the Zorran Sea shores, and later stepped into the beautiful caravans driven by the majestic horses. King Asa's men were there and they soon they were all ready to make another long journey on road, this time all the way to Dora Valley.

Chapter 19
Back Home at Dora Valley

King Asa's men got into one caravan and the Starmen, Akim, Bravo, Sasha, Tara, and King Asa all got into another huge caravan and settled down comfortably on their bunks. Starrho suddenly said to all of them "I have a surprise!"

"What?" demanded Akim, "When will the list of surprises stop? Not that I don't enjoy nice surprises!"

Starrho said slowly, "The Great One instructed us that we can come back to Earth after a week. We have a brief mission, then we will come back to help you distribute copies of the Golden Book all over the Earth. We have to leave Earth tonight to finish another mission, as I said though."

Everyone whooped in delight and shouted, "This is the best wonderful surprise!" and everyone kept beaming happily as if they could not stop. Akim felt joyous and kept grinning ear to ear as if he couldn't stop.

It was a comfortable journey. The seats were soft with many cushions and the caravan had fresh white curtains, which cooled the caravans. The windows were open so cool air filled the caravans. It was a bright blue morning with a few puffy white cotton clouds and many birds chirped happily dancing from tree to tree. The pathways were shady, cool and green, and many streams and springs gurgled along the way. The stallions trotted along the dust roads and stopped often for a delicious juicy crunchy apple for a snack, as it was hard work for them. Everyone was happy, and tired as expected during the last lap of their long travels.

They did stop on the way for food and drink, and rested at night in the caravan bed bunks where all of them slept fitfully. It was a refreshing journey back to Dora Valley, with a lot of sharing stories, laughter and joking. Akim felt exhilarated. He kept the Golden Book in a little white box, given to him by King Asa.

Starrho had told Akim solemnly, "Akim, you are now the new keeper of the Golden Book, keep it carefully and hide it too!"

Akim nodded and said "Yes, Starrho, I realize this Book must be hidden, never stolen ever again as the Green Snake had first stolen it!"

A few days later, they arrived in Dora Valley in the early evening. As they entered the little valley town, Akim got a pleasant surprise. He saw Aunt Nelly coming out of the little supermarket in the valley carrying a basket of provisions.

"Hi Aunt Nelly, we are back, look here!" shouted Akim excitedly and ran to the caravan door.

Aunt Nelly did not seem to hear Akim, but looked up and stared at the caravans thinking, "Fantastic, what grand caravans! I wonder which fancy visitors have come to town!"

In fact, everyone in Dora Valley was staring in fascination at the beautiful caravans.

Akim called out again "Hi Aunt Nelly, here!" The caravans stopped and Akim ran out and on seeing him, all the valley people gave cries of delight.

Aunt Nelly rushed forward to give Akim a bear hug. "Akim, you came back even faster than I thought, this is the best news in weeks! My dear, we need a big celebration tonight!"

She then beamed at the Star Men and said, "Hello again my wonderful friends! You indeed kept your word and brought Akim back as you said and even sooner than I thought; I actually feared I would not see Akim for a year or even more!"

Starrho replied solemnly, "The mission hastened in its time because everything fell in order, everyone did what they had to do on time, and now, much more has to be accomplished!"

Aunt Nelly smiled not quite understanding Starrho's mysterious words.

Mr. Sodo the big burly chief inspector saw Akim, gave a loud whoop and shouted out, "Hello Akim, you look so different and so strong, something great has happened I know!"

Mr. Mundy the principal seeing the crowd gathered around the caravan came to see what was happening and was very surprised and glad to see Akim. He cleared his throat, came forward and shook hands with Akim. "Great boy Akim, you did us all proud, you are an honor to Dora Valley!"

Akim replied grandly "We all did it together, and I did not do much really!"

Zora said loyally, "Akim played the very important role of getting the Golden Book along many other things such as breaking the curse of the bad witch!"

"Golden Book and wicked witch, Akim you certainly had the strangest adventures!" exclaimed the folk in Dora Valley.

Aunt Nelly replied, "Wait for tonight everyone, we will have a great banquet and then let them tell us everything!"

"Good idea!" agreed everyone.

Just then, Mr. Loki drove past in his royal caravan and frowned when he saw the crowd. He was even more annoyed to see Akim and the Star Men along with a group of royal people along with a grand man who wore a crown, all the center of attention.

He came forward and said "Ha! You are back, boy! Hope there will be no further trouble in town with your strange friends. I always warned the town people to stay clear of unknown strangers. They always bring trouble, but sad, no one listened to me!"

Aunt Nelly glared at Mr. Loki and said sharply "Are you not glad that Akim is safe and accomplished an important mission for the Earth, Mr. Loki?"

Mr. Loki snorted rudely and said "Ha! What mission, mischief makers, more likely," and he walked off. The others stared after him thinking he was an extremely bad-mannered man. The valley people felt embarrassed by Mr. Loki's behavior.

"Never mind," said King Asa soothingly. "There are such people as these in the world. It takes all kinds.

We just have to keep doing what we have to do without being bothered by their unkindness."

Akim was grateful for King Asa's graciousness because he felt extremely embarrassed by Mr. Loki's rude intrusive speech.

Finally, everyone forgot about the rude Mr. Loki, as there were many things to get down especially with tonight's banquet preparations.

Akim hastily introduced all of them to the valley folk.

Aunty Nelly then said, "Come on everyone in Dora Valley, banquet tonight under the stars. All are to come. Please call Mr. Loki too and his friends, we do not want anyone to be left out!"

Many groaned saying, "Not Mr. Loki, maybe we can call Mrs. Loki and leave Mr. Loki out!"

Starrho said, "Yes, it is right, we must give Mr. Loki the benefit of a doubt, he should come for the banquet along with Mrs. Loki!"

Everyone was excited and looking forward to the night. Different people of Dora Valley gathered around Akim, and the others.

Uncle Jon had come by now and hugged Akim joyously and welcomed all the others happily. They rested and freshened up. Late in the evening, all the people in Dora Valley gathered in a huge field where they made a gigantic bonfire under the glittering stars.

Then Akim got a big surprise. He had forgotten something. His school bullies! He suddenly noticed them slinking at the edge of the field watching the banquet from a distance longingly.

The bullies were talking among themselves at the edge of the field. Don muttered to his friends "I think Akim will never look at us again. I saw him walk by us and frown."

The other boy, Soki said, "Yes, I saw that look. This is payback time, I guess we will have to go home and eat alone while the whole town is feasting at the banquet."

They were embarrassed to face Akim. Don said, "I see change in Akim. He had a new courage, looks bigger, stronger somehow!"

The boys were convinced that Akim had frowned and walked past them ignoring them, but Akim had not seen them before. He now suddenly noticed them standing at the edge of the field, looking a little anxious and pale in the moonlight with forlorn lost looks and he walked towards them purposefully, with a slight smile.

Then Don said "Oh no, Akim is walking towards us, I think he is going to do something. He must have got some strange powers; he has a strange smile too, mocking smile! "

They tried to walk backwards and their horror Akim reached them very quickly. They all looked at him a little afraid.

Don said quickly, "Akim, we are sorry for everything!"

Akim said "Hello Don, Soki, Jo and Nok!" Don the biggest bully, stared hard at Akim, wondering if he was making fun of them.

They all mumbled a hello sort of looking down at the ground. After a moment, Don looked up and saw in Akim's brown eyes acceptance and not mockery. Don smiled at Akim, almost shyly and then held out his hand to Akim and asked him a little anxiously "Friends?" Don now badly wanted to be friends with Akim. There was something different about Akim.

Akim stretched out his hand gladly, shook his hand and said grandly, "Let bygones be bygones!"

The other "ex-bullies" also extended their hands sheepishly glad Akim had spoken to them. They all made peace with Akim at that moment.

Akim said, "Come on guys, come on to the banquet!" Relieved and happy, the boys joined Akim together to the huge banqueting table and Aunt Nelly looked at Akim and winked.

Don, Soki, Jo and Nok felt a sense of belonging for the first time because all the valley people were smiling at them, and the Star Men, King Asa, Tara, Sasha, Bravo and the others were talking with them. They never experienced people talking with them and just having fun together and this was something new.

The banquet table was loaded with delicious biryani rice, curries, and even steaming hot momos along with soup and after the banquet hot chocolate was served.

Shaan saw Akim, gave a little squeal, and said, "Akim, how wonderful you are back and safe…and guess what, I won the beauty contest, isn't it amazing, everyone said I was the best!"

Akim said, "Hello Shaan, congratulations on your great win!"

Modesty was not Shaan's cup of tea. Shaan sat at the banquet table and kept talking about the contest for quite a while and Don suddenly said to Soki softly, "Shaan is so full of herself, she cannot stop talking about herself and her beauty, I can't imagine why I thought she

was so wonderful. Akim has just come back from a great adventure and she is not even asking him about it!"
 Dendal looked at Don and winked and Don asked Dendal in surprise, "Did you hear me?"

Akim heard that and laughed, and said to Don, "Yes, the Star Men hear what they need to hear, they have very sharp ears and also can read our thoughts when they need to!"
Don smiled and replied, "I actually got the revelation of my life and now I am finally free!"

All the Star Men looked at Don smiling and Don's friends stared at Don, wondering what was happening as they did not quite understand.

That night as all the people in Dora Valley, the Star Men, Akim King Asa, Sasha, Tara and the others sat under the stars, their eyes were shining with joy.

Finally, Akim took out the Golden Book and showed it to them. They all gasped in amazement at its glow and they saw an unearthly light pouring out of it. As they gazed at the Golden Book, it had a mysterious power.

Akim said grandly, "This is the Book of Truth!" The Star Men, King Asa, Akim, Tara, Sasha and the others then proceeded to tell them their adventures, the importance of the Golden Book to stop the work of darkness that was beginning to rule the Earth.

Dendral said, "There is power that is present in the Golden Book, but it can only be received if the Golden Light enters your soul. You have to take those words into your heart and do them, and then the power comes alive. Then, the Light shines on you to give you greater strength. The more you obey; you will start to bring change and wonders around you. In fact, each of you has the potential to change the Earth. A little star can light up the dark. If you do not practice what you read in the Book, nothing much will happen."

After he finished speaking, a group of people sitting at the furthest corner of the bonfire started saying, "We cannot bear that light from the Book, it is hurting our eyes, and it is horrible and dazzling!"

The very rich and powerful man Mr. Loki stood up suddenly and cried out, "I feel sick and giddy looking at the Book, take it away!" Mr. Loki was used to everyone accepting his advice readily but tonight, no one listened to him.

In fact, the Book was very much the center of attention that night and as everyone was busy enjoying the feast, Mr. Loki glared at everyone looking very offended. He repeated again loudly, "I think this is a bad Book, take it away and throw it into the fire!"

"What!" exclaimed everyone in the town loudly, "This could never be done!"
No one had ever stood up to Mr. Loki before and it was too much for him. He stood up in anger and said aggressively, "I contributed money for the new community hall, I gave money for the new stadium, and the new club in the valley. You are ungrateful people. By not obeying me, you have a lot to lose! You are listening to aliens! I am leaving! I warned you about those ridiculous aliens when they had first come to Dora Valley, I told you not to listen to them and now look, they have brought havoc in Dora Valley. Everyone here has lost their senses!"

A group of Mr. Loki's followers also stood up and said, "We are leaving too, it seems the valley is going mad over a silly book and a group of strange creatures

that invaded our peaceful lives. We used to be so happy.
We are leaving this valley first thing tomorrow morning.
We have plenty of places to live in!"

Mrs. Loki said anxiously to Mr. Loki, "Dear don't
leave, listen to what they are saying!"

Mr. Loki gave a withering look to Mrs. Loki and
she shrunk back.
Everyone looked surprised and a little shocked at that
outburst.

Starrho said wisely, "Let them go."

Everyone watched Mr. Loki, Mrs. Loki leave
along with the others and their families angrily, getting
ready to pack to leave the next day.

They were so angry that no one could even say
goodbye to them. They slammed their doors shut, bolted
their doors and closed their windows, drew all curtains
and they started packing their belongings. They spent the
entire night packing, planning to leave in their huge
caravans in the morning. Mr. Loki said grimly, "We will
put up notices for our houses for sale and come back later
for the sale. I cannot stay in this rotten town a moment
longer!"

Mr. Loki and his friends kept grumbling the whole
night as they packed their belongings. They had plenty of
money so they could go anywhere and start up again.

"Cheer up folks," said King Asa, "They are
happier away, and you will be happier too, or they will
keep making trouble for you. Now think of the good
things. We have much to do tomorrow. We have to make
copies of the Golden Book and distribute it through the
Earth."

"Let's sing a song," said the Star Men suddenly.
They started to sing a beautiful song, and a spirit of

exuberance bubbled and overflowed and soon everyone was singing, jumping, even dancing.

In the houses of Mr. Loki, his friends and their families, they all put cotton wool in their ears! They covered their ears with their hands and kept jumping up and down shouting, "Terrible noise, horrible, can't bear it, feeling ill, this is a nightmare, what nasty sound!"

Mr. Loki said, "I am going to get seriously ill with this noise. I just cannot wait to leave, oh give me some more cotton to put in my ears. I need an aspirin too; I'm getting a terrible headache!"

Mrs. Loki gave him a huge ball of cotton to stuff in his ears, a large glass of water and an aspirin.

Their neighbor friends needed more cotton and they gave them more balls of cotton to stuff in their ears. In the transference of the cotton, much of the packing was left undone. In the end, they decided it was impossible to leave the next morning and would need another day to pack. With that, they all flopped down on their beds, ears stuffed with cotton.

Meantime, back in the banquet, the folks were all happy and unaware of the "torture" that Mr. Loki, his friends and families were undergoing with their songs.

Then, the unexpected happened. Mrs. Loki gave Mr. Loki the biggest shock of his life. She suddenly stood up and looked like a lioness and then she said firmly, "Now dear, I think this is going quite far, the Star Men and Akim are here to help us and instead of joining them, we are moving camp, I don't quite agree with what you are doing, don't you think we should join them?"

Mr. Loki looked at Mrs. Loki, his mouth opening and closing like a goldfish. He had never seen Mrs. Loki disagree with him, and now for the first time, she was doing it for the sake of some horrible aliens. He was too shocked to speak and when he finally found his voice he said, "How could you side with them, this is being traitor!"

Mrs. Loki replied firmly, "No dear, I am speaking for the truth and for the right thing. We can move away from Dora Valley, but wherever we go, we will have the same problems, but the Golden Book is given to help us to overcome our problems, please accept it!"

Mr. Loki was flabbergasted and did not know what to do with the new Mrs. Loki who suddenly looked very bold with a glint in her eyes. He was sure that the Star Men had cast a spell on her to make her turn against him, but Mrs. Loki was far too kind to be under any kind of forbidding spell.

Mr. Loki rushed out to his friends' homes to tell them of Mrs. Loki's revolt and they all hurried to Mr. Loki's house indignantly to talk to her. Mrs. Loki stood her ground and said firmly, "My friends, the Star Men are helping us with the Golden Book and we are being foolish to walk away from that help.

Finally, Mr. Loki said, "I think Mrs. Loki is very tired and has lost her mind, she will be okay in the morning, let her sleep it off!"

Mrs. Loki said, "No dear, I am not going to sleep, but to make peace with the Star Men and the others. We have been arrogant with everyone. My dear, money is not everything, look at our hearts, we are not happy."

To the shock of everyone, Mrs. Loki marched out and everyone started at her in amazement. When the Star Men and the others saw her approaching the banquet table, Akim stood up and called out, "Mrs. Loki, come and join us, we are so happy to see you again."

Mrs. Loki came to the banqueting table with a big beam on her face and had a beautiful evening with them. Finally, Mr. Loki sheepishly came out after an hour. Everyone cheered loudly and clapped their hands when they saw him approaching them very weakly, and Mr. Loki suddenly beamed, smiling from his heart for the first time. This was the first time he really felt accepted. Mr. Loki's friends were now furious with him for joining the banquet and refused to speak with him from that day forth.

Mr. and Mrs. Loki had a wonderful time that night at the banquet and Mr. Loki said in surprise, "I could not bear the sight of that light of the Book, but now it looks beautiful and your voices are so soothing!"

Dendal said wisely, "Mr. Loki, when you stopped resisting the Truth, it could reach you, deliver you and set you free and now you are enjoying the wonders of Truth and the Light."

Mr. Loki nodded his head, and Mrs. Loki squeezed his hand, her eyes shining, she had never been this happy in her life.

Mr. Sodo, the chief inspector of police said with his eyes shining, "I have never been happier in my life, I never sang so much before!"

Mr. Mundy, the principal nodded his head in agreement and said, "True, never a more wonderful moment, I never knew there was so much joy in singing, it has its own secret power."

"Yes" said Sheila, the wise lady in the valley, "As we are singing, I am feeling much happier! This has never happened before. This is the best time ever!"

The moment came when the Star Men said goodbye to all, with special hugs to King Asa and his

men, Akim, Sasha, and Bravo and Tara and others. Then,
they were gone, flying up in the beautiful starry night
until they were shining little dots far up and could hardly
be seen.

Aunt Nelly vigorously fanning herself kept saying,
"Well I never!"
Uncle Jon stared up in wonder while the others waved
vigorously and Akim, Sasha and Tara were very silent.

After clearing up after the banquet, everyone
settled to go down to sleep, it was past midnight. King
Asa and his men were to spend the night in Dora Valley's
special guesthouse. Akim and Bravo were in Akim's
bedroom and Tara and Sasha were in the guestroom in
Akim's home. That night Sasha could not sleep. She
knew in the morning, King Asa and his men would be
taking her back to her home. She was glad that they
would meet frequently and happy that the Star Men said
they would be back in a week. She could not wait! She
went to the window and stared up at the sky,

She turned around and saw that Tara too was
wide-awake and said to her softly, "Tara, I have an idea,
please do not go back to your forest home, please stay
with us. I know my parents would love to have you, my
mother also mentioned that to me!"

Tara smiled and said, "Perhaps I can't stay in your
home, but I may buy a cottage and stay in your town, so I
will be near you. I realize I need people around me.
Being alone in the forest for so many years is a very
lonely life. People make life happier and brighter when
we care and share, which I find in all of you!"

Sasha ran up to her and hugged her with joy. She
suddenly realized why she had to come with Tara to the
City of Skilk; it was for such a time as this, so that Tara

would come to the town and leave the lonely forests.
Yes, Tara had gone to the City of Skilk for that as well as many other reasons, which one day they would discover.

Meantime, Akim also tossed and turned in his bed, he could not sleep. He looked across at Bravo who was fast asleep. Akim finally got up and meandered his way round the farmhouse looking for lanterns. He wanted to sit under the stars that night, and read the Golden Book. The Golden Book glistened on the table next to his bed. He had taken it out of the white box because he had wanted to look at it. Starrho had warned him not to keep it out, so Akim was actually planning to make a special cupboard for the original Golden Book. He finally found two oil lanterns in the kitchen, lit them and took them out with the Golden Book. Tiny fireflies danced around him as he made his way out into the garden. The dogs whined and wagged their tails in surprised, wondering why Akim was out at this time. Akim patted them and then set out to his favorite tree, and hung the lanterns on a branch of this old tree, sat under the tree, opened the pages of the Golden Book and started to read:

He read about love; how powerful it was and could change a hard cruel world and spread like a fire, warming up cold, angry and lonely hearts.

He read about forgiveness, how it set people free from chains of anger and pain, and they get new strength and joy when they forgive and how miracles start to happen when people forgive.

He read about peace. When humans practice peace in their lives, it flows like a river through the Earth, bringing healing and joy to all nations.

The secret of accomplishment lies in receiving. When humans receive the Truth in the Golden Book, the

Light shines into their souls to pour fresh understanding and give them the power to do practice its Truths. The secret power lies in practicing what they read and then miracles start to happen.

There was so much more to read, which Akim said he would read the next day. As Akin read on, he felt joy filling him. He looked up to the sky and almost seemed to feel the Star Men watching him and nodding their approval.

Akim asked the Great One in his heart, "What about people who can't read?"
The Great One answered Akim deep in his heart, "The ones who cannot read will have the Light of understanding given to them in greater measures!"

Akim was relieved to hear that and said softly, "Thank you Great One!"
Akim gave a sigh of thankfulness and said looking up, "Thank you dear Star Men for showing us the way and really opening our understanding. I can't wait for you to come back again, and help us to distribute the copies of the Golden Book over the Earth! Return soon dear friends!"

Akim finally went indoors at dawn holding the Golden Book and carefully placed it beside his bed on his bedside table back into the white box and locked it. All in the house were fast asleep. Akim finally fell asleep, a happy smile on his face!

Well, many new exciting wonderful things were yet to begin in a new set of adventures, shared with us in another story!

The End